[THE DEAD ARE MORE VISIBLE]

Also by Steven Heighton

POETRY

Stalin's Carnival
Foreign Ghosts
The Ecstasy of Skeptics
The Address Book
Patient Frame

FICTION

Flight Paths of the Emperor
On earth as it is
The Shadow Boxer
Afterlands
Every Lost Country

ESSAYS

The Admen Move on Lhasa
Workbook: memos & dispatches on writing

ANTHOLOGIES

A Discord of Flags: Canadian Poets Write About the Gulf War
(1991: with Peter Ormshaw & Michael Redhill)
Musings: An Anthology of Greek-Canadian Literature
(2004: with main editor Tess Fragoulis, and Helen Tsiriotakis)

CHAPBOOKS/LETTERPRESS

Paper Lanterns: 25 Postcards from Asia
The Stages of J. Gordon Whitehead

STEVEN HEIGHTON

THE DEAD ARE MORE VISIBLE

STORIES

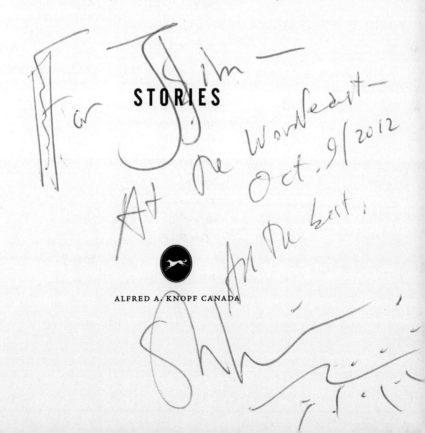

ALFRED A. KNOPF CANADA

PUBLISHED BY ALFRED A. KNOPF CANADA

Copyright © 2012 Steven Heighton

www.randomhouse.ca

Knopf Canada and colophon are registered trademarks.

This book is a work of fiction. Names, characters, places and
incidents are either the product of the author's imagination or
are used fictitiously. Any resemblance to actual persons, events or
locales is entirely coincidental.

Library and Archives Canada Cataloguing in Publication

Heighton, Steven
The dead are more visible / Steven Heighton.

Short stories.
Also issued in electronic format.

ISBN 978-0-307-39741-6

I. Title.

PS8565.E451D42 2012   c813'.54   C2011-907795-7

Printed and bound in the United States of America

2 4 6 8 9 7 5 3 1

For my sister, Pelly Heighton,
and my nieces: Tarah, Christine, and Julia

CONTENTS

Those Who Would Be More 1

A Right Like Yours 41

Shared Room on Union 53

OutTrip 77

The Dead Are More Visible 99

Noughts & Crosses 123

Fireman's Carry 139

Heart & Arrow 153

Journeymen 177

Nearing the Sea, Superior 197

Swallow 209

Notes & Acknowledgements 257

[THOSE WHO WOULD BE MORE]

Now and then, the man and his boss discuss the weather

Principal Eguchi ordered scotch instead of beer. Scotch
for both of us. We were meeting in Brain Noodle, as
we did every week after the Saturday-afternoon cram
class I'd been teaching for her since my arrival in Japan
ten months before. In public like this, she was always
formal with me, but today she was practically rigid and
her English had developed a limp.

"You've promoted us from beer to scotch," I said.

"I have—pardon? Promoted you?"

I knew that Brain Noodle's manager and chefs and
wait staff all considered Principal Eguchi a troubling
phenomenon—a tall, polished woman who owned her
own business and drank quantities of beer in public.
And now *scotch*. She was not sipping.

"A manner of speaking," I said, waiting for her to

slip out her pocket dictionary and demand details. I'd never had a student in Eguchi's school as meticulous about learning English as Eguchi herself, as if she had founded her American-English school simply as a pretext to improve her own grasp of the language. Officially we met each Saturday to discuss the students and any problems that might have come up during the week, but largely these meetings—like our other encounters—were tutorials for her. I didn't mind. My salary was good, Eguchi was intriguing on a number of counts, and the food at Brain Noodle was superb.

Today the dictionary remained in her pearl handbag, though she did snap the bag open to take out her matte silver compact. She wore as much makeup as any woman I'd ever met. It was applied kabuki-style and, in times of stress, fine-tuned in public. She was a good-looking woman and I never saw the point of this hyperbolic rigour, but of course I said nothing.

"Is everything all right, Ms. Eguchi?"

"Would you care for another Suntory!"

"Should we order first?"

She seemed confused. Her eyes were always evasive—she tended to focus on my mouth when I spoke, which usually made me light a cigarette or reach for the toothpicks sheaved in shot glasses along the sushi bar—but today her eyes could find nowhere to land.

"Uh, Ms. Eguchi . . ."

"Some of the parents are compliant," she said in a rush, finally meeting my gaze.

"Compliant? You mean—in sending us their children?"

"They say the children are so happy in the *juku*."

"Oh, oh, you mean 'compliment.' As in—"

"*Too* happy, the children. Too much play, not enough work. These parents are . . ."

I sat back. "Oh. These are complaints."

"Several complaints. More than several. How many is several, Sensei? In English?"

"Well . . . I guess around three or four."

"Ah. How many is many?"

"There've been *many* complaints?"

"They say that recess is half the class, Sensei! That means, two hours or more."

I could only nod.

"And, you refuse to assign the housework."

"Four hours seems like a pretty long time to keep three- and four-year-olds at a desk. On a Saturday."

"You have said this before, Sensei. And I have said: Short recess, no problem. But not like this."

"Some of the children aren't even three yet!" Several. Many.

"Their parents are erecting to send them here. You are paid to teach them."

I thought of how some of the smaller pupils couldn't even understand the simple Japanese I had to use to give instructions. I'd tried before, diplomatically, to convey my feelings about the *juku* to Eguchi; she'd simply told me that Westerners—especially of my generation—could never hope to understand Japan.

"Perhaps I feel I have not given you enough time off," she said, inscrutably.

"Have you told these parents that we learn English *during* the recess?"

"But how, Sensei?"

"Like I said before. I play games with them. They learn to count. They learn verbs."

"English for playing the game is not what the parents want to learn for them."

I had to look away. I signalled the waiter for two more scotches.

"All right. I can try shortening the recesses."

"Thank you, Sensei. But . . ."

"But only by so much."

"But I have *promised* these parents, Sensei!"

She was looking at me in a kind of agony. I had seen this before. She was imploring me to take her meaning so that she would not be obliged to finish her sentence, to strip matters to the root. I decided not to help out. I finally sensed what was going on.

"I have promised to give shrift to their compliance, Sensei. I am very sorry. So sorry." The scotches arrived. The waiter glanced at us sidelong. I picked up my scotch and drank it off, then stood, eyes stinging.

"I gather you mean that I'm fired."

"No!" she said, aghast. "Only that I must replace you at once!"

——

Each day, the child brings to the teacher an apple

A month into my stay in Japan I began to notice oddi-
ties in the primer I had been using to teach myself the
language. I'd bought it in a used bookshop on a cul-de-
sac in downtown Tōkyō. It was close enough to the Ara
River that you could smell the water—sour, swampy—as
you emerged from the cramped interior. The shop was
about fifty feet deep and maybe six feet across—four
feet if you deducted the width of the high shelves on
either wall. I suppose at one time the space had been
no more than an alley between buildings that would
have sprouted from the ruins left by the American air
raids of '44 and '45. I was in a hurry (on my way to
meet Principal Eguchi for the first time: job interview)
and didn't spend long comparing the different primers
that crammed a good three feet of shelf space. I chose
one of the less foxed and fretworn paperbacks: *Japanese
for the Beginners and Those Who Would Be More*. The
authors shown in the discoloured photo on the back—
bespectacled, beaming under a cotton-candy froth of
flowering cherry trees—were professors in Kyōto, a
pair of elderly and venerable linguists. The book had
been published in 1969. I supposed they would be dead
by now. It cost just a hundred yen.

The vocabulary for lesson 1 was unsurprising: *thank
you, pencil, dog, floor, home, why, when, this, that, him, her,
good night* and so on. It was when I started memorizing
the words for the next lesson that I noticed an oddness

[5]

of tone and trajectory. This was a few weeks later, when my honeymoon with the new was waning, giving place to spells of fatigue, commuter claustrophobia, sensory saturation—all the usual markers of culture shock. Among the cats, the cars, the uncles and aunts, houses, doors, windows and other basic vocabulary, the word *shitai* appeared: "corpse." The authors, Drs. Sato and Okubo, then perkily urged me to translate a number of Japanese sentences into English, including *My mother's pencil is on the table, When Father comes home, he sees the good dog,* and *When I looked through the window, there was a corpse on the floor.*

I flipped to the appendix to check my translations. All correct. Then, after a dozen or so other standard phrases, this: *My uncle says that there are some corpses in that house.* Bolder now, I tinkered with the sentence and, seizing some lyric license, settled on: *In my uncle's house are many corpses.* It went on like that. The oddness was diverting enough, but more than once, trying to study while packed among standing, dozing salary-men on trains that were like human trash-compactors, I glanced up and looked around, spooked, like a man reading a tepid letter that swerves mysteriously into threatening tones.

In my second month I moved a backpackful of worldly goods into a midget flat not far from the book-shop and the river. I spent little time there. I ate in noodle shops or sat in the park with a book when I wasn't working, commuting. The flat never began to look lived in. Its vacant echoing never ceased—that audible sign that a tenancy has taken root. I was grappling now with lesson 3, which focused on the use of the past tense and introduced new vocabulary. The Second World War, or some discreetly unnamed facsimile, made its first appearance. I wasn't completely surprised. Among the new words that I committed to memory were *rifle, battle, ruin, bomb.*

My aunt stayed with us here for dinner last night.
The sun was bright that day and the wind was warm.
My uncle has a rifle that he found after the battle.
A rifle is no match for a bomb.

———

I will, I shall, I am going to return

In my last lesson that Saturday, before Eguchi fired me, I'd introduced my students to the future tense in English. It seemed important that the toddlers in the class become acquainted with its nuances. As for the four-, five-, and six-year-olds, the concept would be novel for them as well, since there is no actual future tense in Japanese. *Tomorrow I go to the store. Next week I finish my studies. Before long I go home to Canada.* That was futurity, Japanese-style—simple, logical. By the end of the lesson, and not for the first time, I felt frustrated, mildly ashamed of my mother tongue with all its traps and catches, countless irregularities, fine print, provisos, codicils . . . If Japanese had a clear, military order and concision, English resembled a sprawling civilian bureaucracy. Hard to get a definite answer. Harder to find your way around. Week by week, just as Eguchi alleged, I was extending the children's recess.

Japanese may have been the more logical tongue, but months into my study of it I was still not fluent; when I gave the children instructions in Japanese they would titter and shout out delighted corrections. My best student, Yukon, would approach me at recess or after the class to footnote these corrections with the mild and beguiling pedantry of a six-year-old happily instructing an elder. Yukon was the "class name" her mother had asked Eguchi to have me use when addressing the girl. I could see the word's attraction from the mother's point of view—it was Canadian, yet in sound it was close to several Japanese given names, and easy to say. All sixteen children had been assigned class names, either by their parents (Clint, Rocky, ABBA, Milk Shake, Waylon, The Phantom, Marvin, Miami, Mickey Rourke) or by Eguchi, who favoured the sort of name she found in the chunky Victorian classics she was grinding through to improve her English: Dorothea, Clelia, Silas, Clement, Edmund, and—for two-and-a-half-year-old Toshiko Watanabe, who, you could tell from her lumpy form and cowpoke wobble, was still in diapers—George.

Once the controlled chaos of recess was at its peak, Yukon would often withdraw from the action and skip over to join me by the chain-link fence that separated the schoolyard from a cool, high, sound-swallowing oasis of bamboo, an exhaling green jungle in the heart of Tōkyō. I would be smoking while watching the kids (this was the late eighties, and Japan), seeing how their games would permutate, blind man's bluff into tag, tag into hide-and-seek, intrigued by the brisk negotiations that momentarily broke the flow of play—though the flow, in fact, never really broke, not until I stopped it and herded the class back inside. There was something atomic, or quantum, in this constant, shifting action and repatterning, as if the players were linked so closely to a primal source of energy and motion that they would naturally re-enact it whenever conditions allowed.

Yukon would take my free hand and look up at me in her stern manner, her brow crimped hard under the pageboy bangs, lips clumped together as if ready to scold. Her skin was coppery dark. She spoke with a slow, dignified formality—possibly a personal style, but more likely her way of making sure I got the Japanese.

Sensei, chotto ii kangae ga aru yo . . . "Sensei, I have a little idea. It might help you."

"Is my Japanese improving, do you think?" I would always ask, flicking down my cigarette and swivelling my shoe on the butt.

"It certainly is, Sensei! However, you still talk like a woman."

"I know. My verb endings. I know I have to be less polite."

"And what did you have for your snack today, Sensei?"

A quarter pack of Camels, I thought, but I told her, "A muffin and milk." Often at this point I'd have to break off to holler at one or more of the boys. It might be Clement or The Phantom hunkered down on the head of a smaller child like Rocky—a portly, bespectacled five-year-old who wore a tie and looked like a miniature banker—or maybe it was Mickey Rourke, whose name none of the kids could begin to pronounce, trying to wedge Dorothea into the tiny window of the plastic playhouse. "*Damé yo!*" I would call and stride over, gathering George up in my arms to get her clear of the scrimmage, then bringing her back to the fence and holding her, hoping she would again make it through the afternoon without needing a change.

"Tell me, Sensei, do you have all these games at home in America?"

"Canada. Yes, we have versions of them."

"Please demonstrate." This she would say with commanding gravity, and often I would, though one time instead I told her the story of how, in Mexico some years before, I and the woman I was with and some other travellers, one of whom had children, started a game of blind man's bluff in the plaza of Oaxaca City. Local children began to gather. We thought it was because of the novelty of seeing adults at play, and gringo adults at that, but no, it was curiosity about the game itself. When one of our number, fluent in Spanish, asked if they wanted to join in, they said that they would like to but didn't know the rules, had never seen the game before. Play, we urged, and they did join in, and before long they had taken over, as we adults and two children backed out one by one, winded and laughing. We left them there, playing in the lamplight in the darkening plaza under ancient Montezuma cypresses while their parents looked on, visibly tickled. And now (I told Yukon) what I wonder is this: has their game spread outward from that plaza, all through the state of Oaxaca, maybe across the mountains and into the next state— maybe throughout the country? All Latin America? Wouldn't that be something?

Yukon, still holding my hand, gravely watched her surging schoolmates. She seemed to be giving my story consideration.

"Can you stay and keep teaching us, Sensei?"

George had dozed off, her head in the crook of my neck, a line of yellow drool snailing down my collar and onto the tie Eguchi insisted I wear.

Yukon added, "*Gaijin* sensei are forever leaving."

"I think I will go home for Christmas," I said. "I've been away from home for a few years. Eight years now. Imagine not seeing, say, your parents for that long."

"I hardly ever see my father," Yukon said. "I do see his bathrobe. It's white!" Long pause. "If I might ask, will you see your father at Christmas?"

"Well, actually, no." I released her small, cool hand and felt my shirt pocket for my cigarettes, then remembered George on my shoulder. I took Yukon's hand again and explained that my parents had passed away some time ago.

"I used to have two grandfathers," she said after a moment, then smiled.

"I should be back after Christmas, though."

"Perhaps blind man's bluff came to Japan from *Mexico*," she said with force.

I nodded and made a thoughtful face; I saw no reason to quash the fantasy. It wasn't impossible, after all. And it was good to be reminded that if reprehensible things could spread, spilling outward from their origin to stain the world, better things might spread as well.

Upon meeting, the two conceived an inward affinity

Principal Eguchi had hired me in January. She had asked me to meet her at a place called Brain Noodle. I'd wondered if, over the phone, she'd been mispronouncing "Brine Noodle" or something else, but no. When I entered, five minutes early, she rose from a stool at the sushi bar, her hands brushing her skirt as if bits of food might be clinging there, though at her place there was nothing but a glass of beer and an ashtray with a few butts of exactly even length and a fuming cigarette.

"Welcome," she said, splaying her hands, though not widely or ostentatiously, as if quietly indicating ownership of the restaurant as well as her school. "Please join me."

I was feeling buoyant. I had just arrived from tropical Singapore—where for a year I'd been teaching at an academy expressly tooled to generate dutiful, dream-free logicians—and I was finding the relative cold of Tōkyō reviving right to the marrow. And the rush-hour uproar, the near-slapstick tumult of the streets and subway: welcome changes after the embalmed order of Singapore. Energy is optimism and I was ready to start over, one more time. A fresh start might sedate the fear that my years of travel were bringing me no closer to that place where the heart of life beat strongest, and were instead stealing from me the chance of belonging anywhere. I was about to turn thirty and it struck me as old. Old, at least, to have no connections or home, no woman, no child or even niece or nephew—and young to have no parents. Mine had died in a traffic accident several years before, while I was teaching at an American school in the tea-fragrant foothills of Uttar Pradesh, near Dehradun. Paradise, I'd believed. The news had not found me for several weeks. My older brother and our relatives had not forgiven me, as far as I knew, for being so irresponsibly unreachable.

She was tall for a Japanese woman, fit, smartly dressed. A charcoal skirt suit over a blindingly laundered white blouse. Hair back in a tight chignon. Black frame glasses of a style that would seem hip, youthful, a decade later, but at this point did not. In fact, they seemed chosen to make her look older. More formidably set apart. Her makeup was laid on thickly enough that it was hard to guess her age. Asian adults look about ten years younger than Caucasians of the same age; she looked a little over thirty. Her expression during our meeting and through the months that followed was a repeating slide show of purposeful impatience, contained anxiety, and an openness, kindness, that came in what seemed accidental leaks and which she was always quick to deal with, like something that shamed her—a tampon, a bottle of pills or other sign of carnal frailty—flipping from a purse onto a floor.

Eguchi ordered beer for both of us without asking what I wanted. Hot sake was what I wanted but beer was fine. I was hungry and hoped we might order before discussing terms. She barged straight into them. Talking, she looked me over surreptitiously but steadily, as if interviewing not a potential English teacher but a sketch model or stunt double.

"I have made the schedule for you. Here are your hours."

It should have worried me that she pronounced it "oars." She handed me a neatly typed stack of sheets. Her fingernails were painted cerise, but clipped short.

I scanned the top sheet.

"So it's true, what I've heard—we work Saturdays here."

"So it must be," she said, "for everyone."

"Hmm."

"You will find it the same at each school. And the

Saturday is a half day, with the smaller children. An easy day."

"Oh . . . are small children easy?" I was trying to be droll, to disguise my disappointment, but it sounded almost aggressive.

"Here, yes. Especially if you are not the mother. You . . . don't like children?"

"It depends on the child," I said frankly—an obvious mistake. Since I never settled in any place for long, I'd developed the habit of saying exactly what I thought. I'd come to expect not to know people for long. With her gaze on me narrowing, I made a recovery, as I had to—I had just a few hundred dollars to my name. "But mostly, yes, I like them. I'd even say I admire them, if that makes any sense. And like I said on the phone, I have lots of experience."

She made a close study of my mouth. "You have none?" she asked.

"Pardon . . . ? No, as I said, I have lots."

"Ah! And how many is lots, Sensei?"

"Well . . . it depends what we're talking about. Flights, money, continents . . ." I reached for a cigarette.

"I mean *children*, of course."

"Six or seven would be lots."

"Six or seven! Very good, Sensei!"

I studied her, trying to get a read. She turned to the waiter, frowned, and signalled for more beer. The brisk demeanour seemed certain to rule out any advances by

Japanese men, though her air of professional competence and energy was, to a foreigner of my background, attractive.

"I myself have none of them," she said.

"Oh," I said, "no, I meant that I—"

"But, so it goes, I do have hundreds, at the school. I think they are happy there. But we must work hard."

"*Hai, dozo!*" screamed the waiter, setting down two beers like live grenades and fleeing.

"Is it six, then," she asked me, "or seven?"

I lit my cigarette and offered to light hers. "Well . . ."

"Ah!" she said. "By the way, as tomorrow is the weekend, you'll be starting."

Passive aggressive

Around three months into my stay, lesson 4 introduced scads of more advanced vocabulary, including nouns such as belief, disappointment, delight, stamina, entrails, and lethality. In the next lesson, "Expressing the Tense-Future in Japanese," I was asked to translate a number of sentences climaxing with *Tomorrow at sunrise, they intend to shoot me.* Lesson 5, around four months into my stay, helped me learn to manage the oft-used passive voice in phrases that built on the work of preceding lessons:

Tomorrow it is quite possible that I shall be shot.

Next week, perhaps, it is more likely that I shall be shot.

By the end of next month, at the very latest, I am almost certain that I shall be shot.

The lesson also contained some completely fresh material, like the sentence *Kodomo-tachi made mo korosare-mashita:* "Even the little children were slaughtered."

I was now sure that the authors, consciously or not, were trying to discourage their students from pursuing further study. Perhaps they hoped we would leave the country altogether. At one of my Saturday meetings with Eguchi, I did mention the book and its oddness, but in a subtle way, having learned enough about Japan that I figured specificities would embarrass her. Anyway, I couldn't remember the authors' names, and Eguchi was distracted by business matters, so we let it go.

In the next lesson, toward the end of the rice-planting festival in June, casualties continued to mount and this flashcard narrative appeared: *When the bombs began to fall, there was nowhere for my children to hide. Many children were left without mothers or fathers. All through the night, we searched.*

Ghost in the looking glass

July in the schoolyard, sunlight searing through the breezy peaks of the bamboo to cast moving, ink-sketch shadows onto the asphalt. Yukon canters over and stops, dons a solemn face, takes my hand. A question is coming. In my years abroad I've developed into a decent linguist and my Japanese is now good enough for sustained dialogue.

"Sensei, can *gaijin* have babies?"

"Yes, they can!" I respond with enthusiasm. "That's why there are so many of us."

"I don't see many. Once I saw a black man. I was scared of him, but now I'm not."

"My parents had me, for instance."

"I never did see a *gaijin* with a baby. A real *gaijin* baby."

George is in my arms again, drooling against my neck; generally she requires a nap at some point during our now two- to three-hour recess.

"Then you'll have to go to Canada someday, to see. Maybe I'll go back and you can visit me."

For a moment she's pensive.

"What are bears for, Sensei?"

"For chasing and eating Canadian children. That's why there are so few of us."

"I thought you said that there were so many?"

"Well—I survived."

This Lewis Carroll logic seems acceptable to her.

"I wouldn't be discouraged by a bear," she says.

"Would anything scare you?"

"I suppose an extremely bad dream might. Do you have bad dreams, Sensei?"

"Yes. But I don't remember them."

Silence for a moment.

"Then how do you know you have them?"

"I see their tracks in the morning."

"I dream more when Father is away," she says, "but they're not always bad. But he's *always* away."

"That's why I don't have a baby. Because if I did, I'd be away, in Japan."

Through the looking glass again. She knots her brow. The frown releases in a wide, spirited grin that triggers an answering release somewhere in me. My students' minds offer these brief, sweet truancies from my own.

"Now we're playing hide-and-seek, Sensei."

I look over toward the play equipment. Silas is haunched down on Milk Shake's chest, apparently trying to force a handful of gravel into his mouth. In the distance we hear the *mochi*-cake peddler in his megaphone truck, inching through the streets, playing a mournful, minor-key jingle, like the theme of a funeral home. Tasty, tasty, *mochi*-cakes! The sounds and customs of another time.

"I'll join you," I tell her, "as soon as George comes to."

"We would be so honoured," Yukon says, bowing.

People of the Clock

Along with the sometimes macabre lexicon and phrases in my primer, there were dialogues at the end of each lesson that the student was meant to convert into English. Mostly these were untainted by the professors' growing fondness for corpse-filled houses, moaning amputees, children cringing in bomb craters, executions at dawn.

Rather than translate them, I would flip straight to the appendix to read the English versions. Sometimes I would scribble dialogues of my own in the style of the book. It helped me kill hours on the congested, weirdly silent trains I rode back and forth to Eguchi's school and to another school where I sometimes subbed. I read and studied, if with waning discipline, because there was little else to do but be ogled impersonally or doze off on those cars full of sleepers all nodding, twitching in eerie unison as we juddered along through the gloom of tunnels or the sodium glare of stations. Mornings I was the ghost alone among hurried, solid, purposeful burghers; on the night train back, I seemed the only living thing aboard a funeral train of wraiths.

I was aware of a tidal turn gathering somewhere within. For years I'd been in love with being an outsider. Japan, I thought, should have been my Eden, my eventual bride, and would have been, I think, had I been younger. A place I could feel I belonged forever by virtue of not belonging. Never belonging. Islands always rebuff belonging.

But I was falling out of love with distance, absence.

My favourite moment on the ride "home" to my *tatami* closet: as the train crossed under the river and climbed out of the tunnel and shot into the night, a line of huge neon billboards reared across the river like false-front structures in a midway, luminous, festooned, a corporate phantasmagoria of imagery and Japanese characters and twisted English, all mirrored in the sluggish Ara. On a towering billboard, a wry *gaijin*—seemingly James Coburn—sipped whiskey above a slogan set in Gothic script, as if it were a plug for a prog rock band: OF YOU DREAM, BE HANDSOME CAD, FOR YOU PARTY LIFE AND NIGHTIES OF BACHELOR FUN.

DIALOGUE 7: SLEEPING, WAKING

"Who knocks at the door?"

"Open, it is I."

"Please accept my greetings."

"Are you still in bed?"

"Why, what time is it?"

"It has just struck eight. What time is it by your watch?"

"It has stopped. I forget to wind it up."

"Come, my good man, get up!"

"Morning sleep is so sweet. Please go away."

"I don't know how you can lie so long abed!"

"I have nothing better to do; I shall slumber a few minutes longer."

"But a man's life is so brusque! Come now, up, up, up!"

"Never."

"Then I shall strike you, hence, with my cane."

"No!"

"Have at you, you fop!"

"You are worse than the repeating alarm clock."

———

On the march, he felt fortunate to have come to no harm

Eguchi was training for the Tōkyō women's marathon, coming in mid-November. Sunday mornings I would run with her in the bamboo grove next to the school. The grove was a twenty-acre square with a black asphalt path bisecting it diagonally, and a circular track, a kilometre long, fitting just inside the perimeter. To either side of the narrow paths the bamboo rose in high, hedge-like palisades, so at dusk it was already dark. By day the light was a dim and anaesthetic green, the air almost cool. Where the track came closest to the grove's outer edges, traffic sounds from the bordering streets were loud, yet the streets remained invisible. Eguchi— who confessed that for years she hadn't left the vicinity of her school for more than twenty-four hours at a stretch—would finish these runs by sprinting the diagonal path to Mori Dori and into the school-yard to check on the Sunday-morning class, taught by a gaunt, grim young Texan woman whose students were developing comic drawls, especially on words like *dog* and *house*.

"You are not looking your best this morning, Sensei."

We were on our fourth slow lap. Slow, but detectably

accelerating. The leaf light didn't do much for her complexion either, but at least her face showed no signs of strain. Mine must have. I was hungover. The day before, our weekly "meeting" at Brain Noodle had continued through late afternoon, evening, and on into the night.

In a snug salmon tracksuit with lightning-rod seams, Eguchi ran high on her toes with a silent, gliding gait, smooth but for the steam-house pumping of her arms. The lenses of her wraparound shades turned slowly toward me, seeming to monitor me as coldly as security cameras. Then they slipped down her nose, exposing liquid eyes glinting with irony. "In fact," she said, "you resemble yellow." She slid a finger up the bridge of her nose to push the glasses back into place. On our runs, her English gave up all its gains—the only sign of fatigue she ever showed.

"Look," I panted.

"What?"

"I *look* yellow. You need to let me get more sleep."

"And most of the aliens," she said, "lose weight on the Japanese food."

"It's not the weight. It's the smoking. Slowing me down."

Eguchi smoked nearly as much as I did but it didn't seem to affect her wind.

"Smoking only kills the germs," she said. "In the lungs and chest. It's good for us. Smoking expends the capacity of the lungs."

"I've read that men gain weight. When they're ready to settle."

She laughed huskily, an astonishing sound effect, one that I heard only a handful of times over the ten months I knew her. I turned my head sharply. By the time I brought her face into focus, only the shade of a grin remained.

"What's so funny?"

"Foreign teachers never stay. *Gaijin* never settle here."

"I've seen some," I said, my voice squeezed thin and small. Lap six. Silence but for the sounds of our mutual panting, close and loud in that narrow space. "I've seen some *married*. With a house. Kids."

"Yet in their hearts, home is elsewhere."

"I didn't say *I* was ready to settle."

"No, no. Of course not. Let us now do the wind sprint."

Eguchi seemed to decree these sprints whenever we disagreed—on politics, say, or the way I was teaching for her, especially in the *juku*—or maybe she did it by mischievous instinct whenever I was tired. She surged ahead now, darting with the sleek, silent efficiency of a woodland huntress, me clomping along behind like a puffy old satyr. Her tracksuit was a flattering fit. At last she slowed to a trot. I caught up. While I was still gasping, she informed me that she'd decided I was a romantic in my view of the teaching. "Like that curious German," she said. "*Dō iu hito deshō?* Steinman, *deshō ka?*"

"Steiner. Austrian, I think."

"They are one race, Sensei."

"We read him a bit. Teachers' college. Thought kids shouldn't be wakened too soon."

"Awakened, Sensei—in the morning?"

"Metaphorically. Torn from a dream. Pulled into rationality too soon."

"Childhood is not a sleep, Sensei—not now. There's no time for that. Ah, time!" She brought the back of her wrist to her face and frowned as she read her Swatch. "Now we do a lap at eighty percent of utter speed. Begin!"

Lately I'd been smoking Peace cigarettes, a cheap local brand.

"Not that I'm *happy* about it," she said, raising her voice over the bellows of my breathing. "When I was a child, we spend plenty of time hunting insects with the nets. The fireflies and the *semi*. What is it, *semi*? Not the cricket . . ."

"Cicada."

Cheap and unfiltered.

"Your grasp is improving, Sensei . . . We used to bring them back from the fields and the forest and maintain them in the cage with net for walls. We used to name them and play with them like the pets. Summer nights I woke up and came outside after everyone was asleep. To sit and watch the fireflies fly in their cage."

She would not be willing to speak this way, I thought, if we were face to face.

"It's years before, Sensei. Now, it's necessary to work harder. Everyone here. It's just too bad, but so it must be."

She smiled uncomfortably. The need to work hard was neurotically national; Eguchi's need to maintain her school in the face of throttling competition and despite being a professional freak—a lone woman boss among a million male ones—was all her own. She would not slack or stint where her business, her baby, was concerned. "There's no help for it—so it must be." Her fallback phrase. *Shikata ga nai.* And though I could now see the wisdom of occasional unromantic acceptance, surrender, I could not impose such a rueful wisdom on my students. A child is a romantic or no longer a child.

"Faster, Sensei! Don't stop."

"I need to stop."

"Walk a lap," she instructed. "After, we can walk back to the flat. You can have a bath and a rest again."

"A rest," I said, grinning as I gasped. "Right."

DIALOGUE 9: LOVE & THE ROMANCE

"I am in love with a young gal. I fell in love with her."

"You didn't. You got a fancy. You imagine that you are in love."

"My affection is deep-seated. She has the countenance of an angel."

"You are infatuated with her. Your mind is clouded."

"What? How dare you!"

"You fell into the snare of love. Cupid has snared you."

"Not at all! She has a fine figure, a lovely face, an alluring smile. She has so many personal charms. She walks like a duchess."

"Is that all? Has she good sense, intelligence? Has she good education, good breeding? What of her social position? Has she any big brothers? What kind of man is her father?"

"I know only that I love her dearly. Do not trifle with my love. My life without her would be a life of misery. And what is life without love?"

"You are a shapeless romantic. She may reject you."

"Yet for her, would I chance all."

"Shame on you! Friend you speak non sense."

———

He had come to behave toward the boss
with a befitting respect

"Do you have another book of matches?"

"Here, Sensei, you can light it with mine."

"You can call me Curtis, Ms. Eguchi. I mean, here we are."

"I prefer to say Sensei, even so."

"And you still prefer I call you Ms. Eguchi."

"*Sō desu.* There, you see. So easy to light you up."

Even after nine months of this, it was hard to say when she was joking. Her manner was deadpan. Her voice was even, low, and hoarse. Yet during the day, if the phone by the bed should ring and she grabbed it (and she always would, signalling me to be silent), her greeting voice was the standard public female voice of Japan: a breathless treble full of obliging little hiccups and bubbles, all service and subordination. Then she would hang up and, with no apparent self-consciousness, reassume the femme fatale baritone.

"I think maybe I should go back to my place," I said. "I have to teach at the other school, a sub class, first thing."

"Ah, cheating on the side. Is that the phrase?"

"Close."

"You are welcome to stay, Sensei. Stay another hour. It's early. Here."

I laughed as if being tickled. "You again."

"How is that?"

"Deeply unethical. Hang on a sec."

"There's none more in the pocket, I think. Don't you worry."

"Packet. You're not worried?"

"Stay, just so. There."

"But *gaijin* all have AIDS—that's the rumour. And that we're *fertile.*"

"But I am not, Sensei."

"You mean, at this time of the . . . ?"

"In my life. I did want them when I was young. Quite a bit. They never came."

"I'm sorry, Ms. Eguchi."

"Now, I could not have them even if I could. I'm a business. And a divorced one. Nobody marries such a woman. Nobody even takes her for the date."

Except, I thought, *gaijin*. I wondered whom I had replaced and who would eventually replace me at the school.

"I'm sorry, Ms. Eguchi. I think they're fools."

"*O-seiji desu yo!*"

"No—I'm really not flattering you."

"You're improving, Curtis. Sensei."

"This time I want you to look at me the whole time."

I kissed her eyes and tasted kohl.

To describe one's inner feeling

Genki (GENG-KEE): n. or adj.: phonetically eloquent word for vigour, health, high-spirited energy. "How are you today, Curtis Sensei?" "*Genki da yo!*" I'm well. Excellent. Fit as a butcher's dog. No English word quite substitutes and I know that for the rest of my life, whenever I feel the way I feel today, *genki* is how I'll want to describe it. It's that kind of day: autumn sky swabbed free of cloud, smog, or the faintest vapour, hardwood leaves in full ignition, the sun bestowing heat in a mood of mellow generosity, unlike summer's violent excess. As I walk, heels snapping, from station to school through the bamboo grove in this elating air, I recall similar days, years ago in my own abandoned country. Sounds carry in clear air and at dusk on fall Saturdays you would hear the caroming hollers of boys playing road hockey on distant streets in all directions compassing outward, while we—the kids of our street, at the navel of the known world—conducted our own passionate match. It seemed the whole universe was at play.

Working briskly, I conclude the lesson (Word Order in the English Sentence) after some fifteen minutes and announce that it's recess, which it will continue to be till the end of class time. Few, if any, of the students can tell time, but even they seem surprised that the lesson is over. Nor will I be giving homework. I will not withhold this day from them. The cold rains of early winter, I've heard, will soon arrive.

I agree to be the spinner in a game of *tanuki*. Standing in the middle of the yard, eyes shut, I pirouette on my heels while the children run off. On the backs of my eyelids they register as a sonar map of scattering laughs and squeals. My right arm sticks straight out as I spin. When I come to a stop I open my eyes, yell "Freeze!" Whichever child I'm pointing at is out and stays frozen. Eventually only one child—today Rocky—remains.

I retreat to the fence beside the bamboo grove and lean back and light a cigarette, which I don't finish. The air is that sweet to inhale. On the east side of the schoolyard, under a rank of mature beeches, Yukon crouches, gathering the gold and yellow leaves layered in a windrow against the fence, layers deepening even now as the wind culls further flurries from the boughs. When I emerge some time later from thoughts of lobbing a football with my father in such weather—striving for and never quite achieving that ideal, high-floating, hosanna spiral—I see she's deputized her little acolytes George and Dorothea to help. I break up a minor fight (Edmund Oyama vs. the Phantom), reconvene the kids and organize a game of animal tag (all animal names to be yelled in English), and still Yukon persists with her project. From time to time she glances over, pretending not to look. Clumsy, comic espionage. I smoke another cigarette, this time finishing the job.

People will tell you, "I don't want a child because it just seems wrong to bring a child into a world like this." High-minded horseshit, in my view. A cut-rate cliché. When has it not been a troubled world? People have children or don't have them for their own selfish reasons, and that's fine and natural. No need to dress up the option as a philanthropic gesture.

For a long time I used that same excuse myself. At teachers' college and in the years after, in the States and Mexico and two Asian countries. With several women who were interested in complicating our connections, maybe for worse, maybe better, who could say? It meant the end of those affairs, and now, instead of being generationally webbed into the world—which no longer sounded like a trap—I found myself peripheral, placeless, the owner of an accent nobody could pin down, a citizen of departure lounges and unfurnished rental units.

As I pivot my toe on another dead butt, Yukon slowly approaches. George and Dorothea trail. Something is up. Normally Yukon will run up to me, abruptly stop, take my hand, speak gravely. Now in her cupped and sunlit hands something is hidden. She holds it near her chest with great care and ceremony, as if it's a robin's egg, or a living chick. She extends her hands. They open slowly. I see a yellow rose. She peers up at me with a squint, the sun in her eyes, a shy grin. "Here, Sensei." I bend closer, reach out: it's a rose of yellow leaves. She has foliated the leaves in tight, concentric circles, perhaps around a pinecone or a stone or a plum pit. The full shape and the involutions are convincingly floral. A living flower out of dead leaves. I take it from her gently. A red hair-tie near the bottom seems to hold it together. I grip it there, pinched tightly, to hold it together.

Phrases for emergency

"I am looking for my son and daughter. Have you seen them anywhere?"

"I have not. I have been hiding."

"Hiding! Friend, this is no time to hide!"

"Who would not be afraid at such a time?"

"Only think of the needs of your neighbours! Many call out for your help!"

"I will aid you in looking for your children, then. I resolve to help."

"I am grateful."

"When did you last set eyes upon them?"

"This morning, when they left for the school."

"Where would they have gone at the sound of the sirens?"

"To the shelter, it goes without saying! But the shelter lies in ruin."

"Is there anywhere else they could be?"

"Perhaps in the forest. Perhaps they have hidden there."

"Shall I come to assist in your search?"

"I should be much obliged. I should not like to search for them alone."

"In next to no time we shall find them!"

"Come, let us proceed now."

"We shall. Be of good cheer."

The floating world

I may have been jilted professionally, but not sexually, not yet. On Monday, when I went into the school to empty my small desk—and to inform Eguchi that I would be flying to Canada within the week and would need my final paycheque before then—she suggested, awkwardly but frankly, that I should stay with her at least a couple of times before I left. In spite of the firing, I was too amused, and maybe flattered, to turn her down. Men are easily flattered; I should have seen that she was merely feeling in advance the loneliness of a vacant bed. She would not have admitted that she hated sleeping alone, but I knew it. Always, after the night's last sex and cigarette, we would turn away from each other and lie back to back, space between us, to fall asleep, but when I woke up in the small hours she would be furled into me, face on my shoulder or pressed into my nape, sleeping hard.

Actually—be honest—I felt the same way about sleeping alone. Actually, in my sleep, I did the same thing as she did. Pressing myself into her, my heart full.

On a cold night of rain, the prospect of a good dinner and drinks and then sex and twined sleep—belly pleasures shared with a keen partner—stirs an expectancy under the heart that's a facsimile of real love. For drifters and outsiders, that may have to do. The night before my flight out, we had an excellent dinner at Brain Noodle, hot sake, appetizers, sashimi and *chanko nabe*, all on her yen, then I walked her home through the rainy streets, sharing her umbrella, which I held. She slipped me a windowed pay envelope as we walked, hips jostling. "I thought it would be better to give it to you now, rather than afterward . . . after tonight. In the morning." Behind her fogged glasses her look was as deadpan as ever, but her tone was distinctly droll. I laughed, a little drunk. I took the envelope and said, "I can't stay until morning, though. I wish I could. I still have some packing to do and I have to be at Narita at ten."

That night the sex sustained itself not just on the knowledge that this wouldn't be happening again, but also, I felt, on a covert fuel of aggression. She slammed her body against me, worked me mercilessly with her mouth, refused to let either of us rest, all the while locking me into a sexual staring match that was unnerving after almost a year in Japan, where I was no longer used to maintaining eye contact for more than a second, even with her, a lover. Now her gaze was more like an assailant's. *You forced me to fire you*, her eyes seemed to say. *I didn't want to. I wanted this to go on. But my school is too important to risk.* I found that I was angry too, my bites and sucks and thrusts and clutchings all forceful, rough. A firing *is* like a jilting; even if you fully understand the reason, in your gut you feel panic and anger.

For a long while we couldn't exhaust that anger and desire, but at last, after an orgasm that for me was almost painful, as if pulled into being by the roots, I collapsed and we lay side by side, staring into space, for now too tired even to smoke.

"I'll need to go now," I told her. "Soon, anyway."

Her voice was amused: "Go means 'to come,' you know. In Japanese we say 'to go.' *Iku.*"

"I think you told me that once. They don't mention that in my primer."

"I suppose you will forget your Japanese."

"I don't think so—not anytime soon," I said honestly. "You'll remember to say goodbye to my students for me? Especially the Saturday kids?"

"Of course. I'll say that you are called off by a family emergency."

"Which is hilarious. I have no family."

"You will have."

I propped myself on an elbow and looked at her—she did not look back—and it struck me that she was right. Somehow she knew it and, just then, so did I. The facsimile of love, however convincing, would no longer do.

I lay back down, emptied, my whole body in a flaccid state.

"I won't forget all my Japanese," I said, staring down at my pale paunch, still growing despite all the running and sex. "I'll always remember how to say 'corpse.'"

"Ah, yes, your lesson book. You asked. I intended to tell you. I know the one."

I turned to look at her again. In the near dark I could see how the makeup had smudged around her eyes.

"There was a scandal about that book. I was at a university then and people spoke of it. One of the professors was an officer at the war, and afterward he was imprisoned by the Americans, I can't recall the reason. But the other professor, Okubo I think he was named—"

"That's it—Dr. J. Okubo."

"He was *against* the war. He was a pacifier, in the university. So, he was imprisoned as well, but throughout the wartime, by the imperial government. And then in the big firebombing, his wife and children were killed. I can't recall how many children now. Maybe not his wife. But the children, yes—maybe three. It changed him. And the later bombings too . . ."

"Hiroshima," I said, "and . . ."

"*Sō desu.* He began to write books, history books, novels and the poetry, even this language book you use. He said Japan was not the aggressive one, but a victim. At the American occupation, they called him the white-washer and forced him to depart the universe."

"University."

"Of course. But he kept on writing."

"I suppose Japan *was* a victim," I said. "You can be a bully and a victim."

"Aliens would weaken the purity of the Japanese race and culture, he believed. He believed the aliens should not remain here." She paused for a moment. "I think that both of those professors have now passed along. I have not heard of that book for a long time. Difficult to find, I think."

"I've gotten to like it. Most of the time, it seems completely normal."

"That's Japan," she said.

"That's any place," I said.

We fell asleep and I only woke at dawn, with Ikuko (her first name, which, out of respect for her wishes, I never used aloud) wrapped around me. She was warm and smelled wonderful. It took some time to disen-tangle myself so I could get up and clumsily dress and rush out to hail a cab to the station. She didn't see me to the door. Nor did she say goodbye. As the gloom of a wet December dawn crept through the apartment, she pretended to sleep, her face turned into the pillow and hidden by her hair and her hand.

Lesson 12

As the sun rose on that summer morn, the city lay in ruin, with the dead all about. The survivors felt a loneliness so great, words may not describe it.

Omoikiru

On the long flight east over the Pacific, passing under the sun and abridging the day, then the night, I skimmed through the final lessons of *Japanese for the Beginners and Those Who Would Be More*. I was exhausted, but sleep was nowhere. At one point I took Yukon's rose of yellow leaves from my carry-on bag. I was trying to keep it fresh in a baggie; it was already starting to wilt. On airline postcards showing a tiny 747 leading a vee of Canada geese across a clear autumn sky, I wrote a note to Eguchi and, care of the school, to Yukon.

The professors' final lesson was equipped with the usual vocabulary lists, lexically obsolete dialogues, and ordinary sentences alternating now and then with odd ones. *The living mourners remained, yet the house seemed empty with the corpse gone off.* Now and then I was distracted by the in-flight film—*Working Girl*—but as I reached the book's last pages, my attention quickened at the sidebar definition of a verb I'd encountered on several occasions, never grasping the meaning. I'd meant to ask Eguchi about it. *Omoikiru*, the sidebar explained, is a compound verb formed out of the infinitives *omou*, "to think," and *kiru*, "to cut." *Therefore, "Omoikiru" has the meaning: "to cut off all thought of something"; "to surrender the hope"; "to resign oneself to the inevitable."* I put my head back, closed my eyes and wondered—what else?—how I and billions of other non-Japanese speakers had ever gotten by without the word. *For example: To see again those I have cared for is impossible; there is no help for it but to "cut off all thoughts."*

[A RIGHT LIKE YOURS]

He is short but he has shoulders and I think he wears the flattest shoes going, cheap sneakers of some kind, and that is attractive, that he doesn't try to elevate himself in any way. His look is shy though, maybe cold, with green eyes that don't meet your eyes but look at your mouth or chin in the same way as, when you're in the ring, the other girl will stare a little below your eyes. So maybe he does it to practise. Always be in the ring, Webb Renton tells us.

I choose to think he is just somewhat shy.

It started because I was training for my fifth fight and my sparring partner had hurt that ligament in the knee that's called, I think, cruciate but we just say crucial because that's what it is. The other girls at the club are either on the little or the huge size and Trav is about the same weight as me, though he is shorter, and toward the end of a workout Webb yelled at him to get in there and give me a couple rounds. Trav's face then—like someone told him to throw himself on a grenade. People started gathering ringside. Like I said, it was the end of the night, and I would have been interested too. I don't think the coach had ever put a girl and guy in to spar that way.

So the bell sounds, he comes out as if being shoved from behind and he is ogling my chin as usual, as if meaning to clock me there, but his eyes don't have that focused, violent shine. He sets his hands high with the forearms upright in an old-fashioned stance and he peeks from between them like he's behind bars, a guy who just woke up in jail and has no idea how he got there. I fling a few jabs at his face to see what he will do, which turns out to be nothing, so I hook low to his gut and then I follow with a loaded right and there's this sound like an air mattress just sprang a leak and he takes a seat on the canvas and looks down at his lap with a puzzled frown. In a way it feels good that I've knocked down such a solid and experienced little guy, but mainly I feel bad. He was not trying. "Get up, send something back at her now, she's training!" yells Webb from my corner. Trav's cheeks inflate with air, which he now puffs out through his mouth in a serious way, and he gets to his feet slowly and we begin.

Next day I see him downtown after my shift at the Ramada, where I work in the office. He is walking out of a camera store looking down at some photos and he has this warm, wide-open smile, just the opposite of his awkward frown last night in the ring. I stand in his path so he will have to collide with me or else stop. He stops, looks up from his photos. The smile dies. He'd looked beautiful before, thinking no one could see.

"That's a shiner, all right," I say idiotically, even pointing. "Nice photos?"

He mumbles something and he's not staring at my chin but into my eyes! Well, my left eye.

"Damn," he says now. "Sorry."

"You know what Webb says about fighters apologizing."

"That's just in the ring. I never gave a girl a black eye before."

"Yours is blacker," I argue. "And I dropped my left."

He nods and develops a thoughtful frown. "It's a bad habit."

"Not anymore. I won't drop it in my fight and that's thanks to you."

The shiner is a sexy touch on him, like a pirate eye patch on a pretty-boy face. I think he wants to leave but I would like a few more seconds here.

"Your photos turn out?"

His face unfists, almost smiles. My knees waver like from a scoring blow.

"Sure," he says, "they're fine."

"They of you in the ring?"

"Family," he says, shaking his head. He looks down

at his shoes, which I notice he always does after he answers a question, like he's hoping that when he looks up again you won't be there.

"Parents?" I can't believe how nosy I am being.

"Uh, kids. Son and daughter. Four and three."

I stare from his face to the stack of photos and back again. I cock my head. In a slow, wary way he passes the top photo toward me like he's surrendering his credit card to a mugger. It's Trav, no shiner, pushing his grinning face (!) between the faces of the little girl and boy who are laughing in a wide, stretchy way on either side of him. There's a cake too. The girl's face has been made up as a black and orange butterfly. The faces are a bit blurred, and the pupils are diabolically red, but there's no missing the joy here.

"Birthday?"

"Nicole's third. At the five-pin lanes up on the base."

"Beautiful," I say. "You look young to have a family. I mean, kids."

"Boy came when I was eighteen."

He shuffles. I think he knows what I want to ask.

"It's a shared arrangement," he says, and the look on his face is like somebody tricked him into speaking.

It can be as tempting to hit a face that attracts you as to hit one you hate, if the liked face is not replying to your attraction. At the Friday night workout we spar three rounds and he again pulls his punches but not too much now. A couple times after I score on him he

retaliates instantly and for a second there is an exciting gleam in his eyes and he almost meets my gaze.
He avoids hitting me in the chest guard, though.
Breast shots really kill, so I guess I could see this as a
sign of budding affection, though I realize it might just
be courtesy.

After, I ask if he will walk me to my car and he
growls, "With a right like yours, a chaperone's the last
thing you need." He walks me anyway. We cross the
parking lot and he slows up as we approach each car,
then glances at me as we continue.

"Farther," I say. "I parked over there." I nod up the
dark service road toward the beer store on the far side
of the diamonds.

"Why so far?"

"The lot was packed when I got here," I lie.

"I've never seen this lot packed."

"And like Webb tells us . . . got to fill those legs up
with mileage before a fight."

Several hours later, it feels like, he says, "I think
you're ready. Guess you'll taper back on the sparring,
next couple weeks?"

"Oh I don't know," I say quickly. "That'll be Webb's
call."

The service road lacks lighting. I glance over but
can't read his face. I have butterflies, like before a
fight, and it makes me walk faster though I am trying
to slow down.

"Maybe when you're training for your next fight,"

I blurt out, "he'll put us together again. Give you some extra rounds!"

"I doubt it," he says. "I mean, I'd be *training*."

I will knock him down again next week. He is short and pale and uncommunicative. He needs a shave. When we clinched tonight, he smelled of, I think, garlic bread.

Now he mumbles, "That was rude of me. Sorry."

All of a sudden we're at my ruin of a Lada, which I parked under a crackling amber streetlight in a corner of the beer store lot. It sounds like a zillion volts are running through this light. I know the feeling. There is a ticket under the car's front wiper. Trav removes it carefully and hands it to me with a sympathetic frown. He looks almost apologetic.

"Can I give you a lift?" I say strongly.

"I don't want you to go out of your way, Trina."

"It's no trouble! Get in! Don't mind the mess."

There is no mess. This morning I vacuumed and lint-picked the interior and before the workout I took the car through a carwash where the asshole attendants actually offered me rain gear and then (I watched them in the rear-view) bent over laughing as I drove slowly in.

"Thanks," he says, and my heart seems to trip—then he says, "but I'll walk. Like you say. Got to get mileage into these legs."

"Yup," I say with an idiot's grin. "For sure. That's very true."

I renew my oath to knock him down Monday.

"Anyway, I live close. Near the No Frills." He points in a vague way, like he is embarrassed to live in the neighbourhood, or he just prefers not to locate himself too clearly.

Webb says I headhunt too much and he needs me to work on my body shots. He also thinks Trav needs to work on *taking* body shots if he is serious about turning pro. For a round at the end of each workout he makes Trav become a human punching bag and sics me on him. Trav never looks pleased about these dates of ours. He leans back on the ropes with his blue gloves by his scrunched-up face, elbows glued to his ribs, and my job is to find openings and work his body. He is permitted to move but not to punch, which basically means I can have my way with him. Since he is short, with long, thick arms, it can be hard to find undefended parts of his flesh to pound and I am very careful about not hitting below the belt—though at times I get the urge. Sometimes I feel him flinching, too. He must be concerned that even one of my hard punches could land foul, by accident or otherwise.

Tonight he smells of, not garlic bread, just bread. He works in a bakery, four in the morning till noon, five days a week. He likes it there. He was just promoted. It is easier to pry personal information out of him now and I am getting opportunities because after the last two workouts he has let me drive him home.

To extend the drive, since his place is only a few blocks from the gym, I park some distance in the other direction on the service road, which also means we get to walk first to my spotless wreck of a car. Naturally he is silent on these outings and I have to talk for both of us. I think maybe he is annoyed about the extra walking but he still does it with me and I choose to see this as hopeful.

We are filling our legs with mileage.

When my arms get too heavy to plant the punches Webb is yelling at me to throw, I have no option but to lean in on Trav and clinch, for a pleasant rest. Would anyone notice if I sampled the fresh sweat on his neck? I think Trav would notice. Tonight for the first time *he* initiates a clinch. On Webb's command I have been throwing repeat right hooks at his solar plexus, trying to pry through his guarding elbows, and now I do get through and his stomach is solid, though with a slight layer over it, I guess from all those baked goods. It's so satisfying to connect. He grunts and gasps softly and sags and envelops me and my punches stop dead. He is humid, panting. Webb hollers at him to break and get back on the ropes.

My roadwork is a forty-minute run each day at the traditional hour for fighters in training. It's a struggle to get out of bed but once you are up and out, you can sprint straight down the middle of Princess Street if you want to. I do that sometimes. I have been known to sing at the top of my lungs while doing that.

I would like to sing at the top of my lungs this morning but this morning I will play it cool because *this morning Trav is running with me.* It's the first day of his weekend, Tuesday. You'd think he would choose to sleep in but he says he is used to getting up for work and besides he wants time to get his place ready for his kids, who stay over on these days. Runs With Man is his morning alarm, he says. Runs With Man is a pound rescue dog, Jack Russell and malamute, a furry barrel with a wolf's head and stub legs who trots at Trav's side without a leash.

I would feel more encouraged by Trav's presence if he hadn't said, when I asked him to run with me, that Tuesday is his "usual day for a run anyway."

Like I say, I love running through the city in the last dark with the streets wide and empty and all to myself, but this morning after we do some of that, Trav asks me to run across the causeway to the fields and hills around the old fort. "The sunrise," he says and it sounds like a romantic proposition maybe, except as usual he mutters it from the side of his mouth. But we run across and there's this mist on the river from the night's chill and with the lake still warm from the summer. "Let's go," he says, and frowns at his watch. He has a good idea of exactly when the sun shows its face every day because he works at an east window, and to me there is something so appealing about a guy who sees every sunrise.

We put on a surge as we run up the middle of the road that climbs to the hilltop fort. Trav's face knots up with the strain. When we get there he is winded. This embarrasses him, I think—that he is somewhat unfit or maybe that I am fitter. He mumbles that he can't get out for runs more than once or twice a week, because of his hours.

Runs With Man flops on the grass and his tongue lolls like a pulled muscle.

"So are you really going to turn pro?" I ask, hoping the question won't offend.

"Coach still wants me to, but there's no way," he tells the patch of dirt at his feet.

To my surprise his words are a relief. To my greater surprise I realize I am not serious about turning pro either, though I have talked about it like I am.

"I saw a couple friends turn pro," he says. "Used to think it might be a way to support the kids. Not a chance." He turns to watch the coloured clouds at the horizon as if trying to figure the odds on our sunrise. To me, the view up the river and west over the big lake is enough. This view of Trav in profile is enough. He says, "I'm not good enough to win big prize money and not bad enough to get work as a bleeder for rising stars."

"They love you at the bakery, though."

"For some reason I'm good at it."

I shift my feet downhill so my eyes are at his level, even a bit lower. Will this help? I am almost ready to suggest we start back down the hill when he taps the dog in the butt with his shoe and says, "Go, boy, get that squirrel." The dog's ears prick up and it pelts away downhill toward the water.

"I didn't see a squirrel," I say.

He looks me plumb in the eye and shows his still-good teeth and steps toward me. The sun is up. Clouds are in the way but sunlight sneaks through a momentary opening and it is enough to turn the grassy hill and the fort and the calm river and lake a rosy gold, like in a religious poster. Then it's gone and I am glad because I see that the flush in his cheeks and spreading up to his hairline and down to his throat is not a reflection of the sun at all.

Like Webb says, the one that gets you is the one you don't see coming.

"Just wanted us to be alone for a second," he says, and as I open my arms the hill pulls him down to me.

[SHARED ROOM ON UNION]

They were parked on Union, in front of her place, their
knees locked in conference around the stick shift, Janna
and Justin talking, necking a little, the windows just
beginning to steam. We'd better stop, she said. I should
go now. It was one a.m., a Thursday night turned
Friday morning. Squads of drunken students were on
the town. So far nobody had passed the car. *Hey, take
it to a Travelodge, man!* Nights like this, that sort of
thing could happen—one time a rigid hand had rammed
the hood, another time someone had smacked the pas-
senger window a foot from her ear, Justin's fingers in
her hair stopping dead.

I won't miss this part, he told her.

I really should go, Jus.

Friday was her "nightmare day," a double shift at the

upstyle café/bistro where she was now manager. Thursday nights she insisted on sleeping at her own place, alone. Sleep wasn't really the issue, he sensed. This seemed to be a ritual of independence, and he knew she would maintain it strictly, having declared she would, until they moved in together in the new year. Other nights of the week they slept at his place or hers. They would be moving into a storm-worn but solid Victorian redbrick bungalow, three bedrooms, hardwood floors, in a druggy neighbourhood now being colonized by bohemians and young professionals. Justin and Janna were somewhere on the chart between those categories. In March they planned to fly, tongues somewhat in cheeks, to Las Vegas to get married.

These separate Thursday nights, this symbolic vestige (as he saw it), tore him up in a small way. He could never take in too much of her. He had never been in this position before—the one who loves harder and lives the risk of it. It hadn't been this way at first. Then it was this way, then it wasn't, and now it was again, but more so. This must be a good thing, he felt—this swaying of the balance of desire—and he would try to work out in his mind why it was a good thing, and the words "reciprocal" and "mutuality" would pop up from somewhere, and the idea of a "marital dance," which he thought he had probably read somewhere, yes, definitely . . . and his mind would start to drift, unable to concentrate on the matter for so long, and he would simply want her body next to his again. For now, no excess seemed possible.

Okay, he said. I know.

I'll see you tomorrow, Jus.

Great.

From somewhere the remote, tuneless roar of frat boy singing. Possibly the sound was approaching. One of the ironies of existence in this city of life-term welfare and psychiatric cases was that the student "ghetto," on a weekend night, could be as dangerous as any slum north of The Hub or in the wartime projects further up. She tightened her eyes and peered through the misty windshield. She had a vertical crease between her brows and it would deepen when she was tired. That one hard crease; otherwise her face was unlined.

What's that?

The boys seemed to be receding, maybe turning south toward the lake. Then another sound—the flat tootling ring of a cellphone, as if right behind the car. Still in a loose embrace they looked back over their shoulders. Someone was there, a shadow, as if seen through frosted glass, standing by the right fender.

What? Yeah, but I can't talk right now. Right, I'm just about to. What's that? Yeah, I believe so.

I'd better go, she said.

I'll walk you in.

It's okay, she said. She didn't move.

Call you in five minutes, the voice said in a clumsy, loud whisper. *Me you, not you me, okay?* The shadow wasn't there by the fender. There was a rapping on the driver's side window, a shape bulking. Justin let in the clutch and pinched the ignition key but didn't twist. With his free hand he buffed a sort of porthole in the steam of the window. That middle-class aversion to being discourteous, even to a lurking silhouette at one in the morning.

Open it, the voice said roughly. No face visible in the porthole. Justin twisted the key.

Don't!

Jus, he's got something, stop!

It's not a fake—open the fucking door. The man clapped the muzzle to the glass. Behind the pistol a face appeared: pocked and moon-coloured under the sodium street-lights, eyes wide and vacated. A too-small baseball cap, hair long behind the ears, dark handlebar moustache.

Justin got out slowly, numbly, and stood beside the car, his eyes at the level of that moustache. The man put the pistol to Justin's chest. An elongated, concave man. Some detached quarter of Justin's mind thought of an extra in a spaghetti western—one of the dirty, stubbly, expendable ones. A hoarfrost of dried spittle on the chin.

Janna was getting out on her side, he could hear her.

Just give him the keys, Justin.

There.

And your wallet, the man said. Nice keychain. And your bag, ma'am. Come on.

Ma'am, he'd said. Justin dug for his wallet. His

fingers and body trembled as though hypothermic. The
night wasn't cold—mild air was lofting up from Lake
Ontario and Justin smelled the vast lake in the air, a
stored summer's worth of heat. The pupils in the man's
pale eyes were dilated with crystal meth, or coke, Justin
guessed, aware again of that aloof internal observer—
that scientist—though actually in his life he was impul-
sive to a fault and in his work he progressed by
instinctive leaps instead of careful, calibrated steps. He
lacked focus but he had energy, good hunches. Two
years past his Ph.D. he was in medical research at the
university, assisting in a five-year study of fetal alcohol
syndrome. No shortage of study subjects in this city.

The pistol looked small to him, maybe a fake, but
his knowledge of weapons was vague. He gave his wallet
and then, with a sudden instinct to politeness, reached
across the roof of the car and received from Janna her
olive suede handbag—to pass it to the man. Janna's
crease was sharply incised, her green eyes tight and
stony. No plea for heroics there. She looked dazed and
indignant, he didn't know at whom.

The man got into the car. Justin, as if waiting to be
dismissed, stood by the door as it was pulled shut. Your
door too, the man told Janna—the voice gone thinner,
higher. She shoved it to, the door bouncing back open—
the seatbelt buckle. Don't slam it that way! he yelled, a
man now sustaining an affront to his property. She got
the door closed. Frozen, Justin and Janna meshed glances over the roof. The man was trying to start the car.

Something wrong there. On stiff, stilt-like legs, Justin
edged around the back of the car toward Janna—Janna
retreating, as if from him, though more likely toward
the door of her building.

The man swung open the car door and shouted,
What kind of vehicle *is* this, man?

It's a Volvo. Volvo 240.

I mean what's its *problem?* The man sprang out of
the car and stood teetering by the door, across from
them now, eyeing them with ice-clear but unfocused
eyes. Possibly drunk as well. He flapped the pistol in
the air as he talked in his breathy, squashed tenor. Justin
glanced around. The streets were empty.

I don't know, Justin said. It's a standard. You don't
drive standard?

His assumption that a townbilly would know how.
Pickup trucks and so on. The man's brow clenched, as
if at some inward struggle. Drunk too, yes.

Why didn't you *tell* me?

Well, Justin started. The word soaked up whatever
breath he had.

I can't drive fucking stick!

Oh, Justin said, eyes on the wagging pistol. I'm sorry.

I hardly ever drive, the man said, quieter.

It's all right, Justin said.

Just leave the car, Janna said, monotone, a digital
voice on a recording. You've got our stuff.

The man's cellphone went off like a siren.

Stay there, both of yous.

The pistol aimed vaguely at the space between Justin and Janna. Justin wanted to bridge that space and at the same time move as little as possible. The man had the cellphone to his ear. Janna was rigid. She was a quick, fidgety type—frozen that way she was not herself, a wax replica.

Right, but I said I'd call back. How's that? I don't know why the fuck the thing hasn't come, you call them back yourself! I know, I know, that's why I said don't use them anymore, didn't I? Yeah. That's right. And pineapple on just half this time, right? And don't call back. I might be longer, there's no car now. No, I don't want to now. I'll deal with it.

He jabbed the cellphone into his jacket. He looked to either side.

Into the trunk, both of yous.

What? Justin said.

The man flicked the key over the roof of the car. It slid off the near side and plinked down among the leaves and rotting oak mast along the curb.

Hurry up!

Just take our stuff, you don't need to—

Panicking, the man trained the gun on them over the roof of the car, straight-armed, both hands on the grip, a cop at a police car barricade. They might be dead in a second and the afterimage Justin would take with him into oblivion would be from prime-time television.

Open the trunk!

Okay.

I've got to fucking *walk* now.

Still thinking and seeing with a weird clarity, Justin bent down for the key and as he stood up he studied the keychain in his hand. A tiny plastic bust of Elvis. A gift from her, last Valentine's Day. He walked to the trunk and opened it. This was all right, though. There would be people passing, and the trunk was spacious, as trunks go. The guy wasn't taking them into an alley and shooting them. And though Justin had forgotten his cellphone tonight, he knew that she had hers, she always did, and maybe it wasn't in her handbag now, sometimes she kept it in her jacket.

I'm not getting in there, Janna said.

Get in, the man whispered.

No, I can't, please.

Janna, please.

Stop! she hissed in a private way, straight at Justin, her eyes round with rage.

The man's skinny arm pushed her toward the trunk and she gasped. Justin, flat-palmed, shoved at the caved chest under the denim jacket—did it without thinking. The man swung the gun and the butt cracked Justin in the side of the head. He saw a screen of blue light, heard a fizzing sound like static or a can of beer being opened, as he sat back into the trunk. A sick, cold feeling, nausea in the bones, plummeted down his spinal column to his toes. Beaten, he tucked up his dead legs and curled obediently into the trunk. She was making a faint blubbering sound as she climbed in after him. No, I won't, she said as she climbed in. I can't. Please.

Get in, Justin and the man said at the same time. Now just move your foot, the man told her, his voice still quiet but in a different way, maybe appeased, maybe appealing for a sort of understanding. The trunk was deep. It snapped closed and after a second there was a sound of steps running off. The sound-space between the strides was long and Justin had an image, projected on the sealed darkness around him, of the man loping away up Union, long arms dangling, almost simian, mouth slack and panting under the droopy moustache. In their politically civilized circle, people didn't use words like "trash" or "skag" about the distressed elements—addicts, parolees, the generationally poor— who made the city's north side seem more like a slum in Jackson, Mississippi, than part of the old limestone capital of Canada. But now in his anger the words occurred to him. And what he should have done. What he would be doing mentally for weeks to come, rewinding the scene, re-cutting it.

Fucking yokel. Cops will have him by tomorrow. Are you all right?

No. She expelled the word on a faint puff of breath. He was groping in the dark for her shoulder. He found her breast instead and she seemed to recoil, though there was no room for that. In the deeps of the trunk, furled on their sides in mirror image, they lay with knees pressed together, faces close. Her breaths, coming fast, were hot, coppery, sour.

Janna? He found her shoulder and she didn't move.

She said, Could air be running out already? I feel like it is.

No, no way. And the car's ten years old. We'll get some air in here.

I don't feel it.

Breathe slower, he said. Do you have your cell?

In my bag. It's gone. I didn't want to get in. Why did you just get in?

I didn't. You saw, he smacked me. I was out for a second. He would have shot us. My head is—

I can't be *in* here, Justin. I can't! You knew that, too. That I'm claustrophobic.

He'd never seen her this way. Even in private she was always capable, composed, professional, as though feeling herself under constant scrutiny by some ethical mentor. Too much so, he sometimes felt. How she would never miss a day's workout in the spring and summer while training for her annual triathlon, whatever the weather or her, their, schedule. How she would talk of getting "more serious" about the sport next year, maybe doing more events. Even her recreation—nights out, parties, vacations—she undertook in this same carefully gauged manner, pacing herself. Only so much fun. Only this much frivolity and no more. As if she was afraid of some tipping point.

Till now he had not let on to himself how her

discipline—what he had so long lacked and craved—
was coming to irk him.

I've told you I'm claustrophobic. Why didn't you tell
him?

He probably wouldn't have known the word. Christ,
my head.

Of course he would know it.

And I didn't *know*. I mean, I thought you were just
saying that before. Everyone says they're claustrophobic.

I don't even like when you pull the quilt over us!

To make love, he thought, in an exclusive cocoon,
cut off from the world.

I'm sorry, Jan, he said. The throb in his head was
worsening and something was gouging into his hip.
Maybe a tool? Something useful here? Of course there
were no tools in his trunk. He felt the thing, an old
ballpoint pen. His mouth was parched.

And I really have to pee, she said.

That's just nerves, he said. His own guts were wheel-
ing. But it calmed him somewhat, being the one in
control like this, consoler and protector.

What's that?

A car revved past, humping out a heavy rap number,
the octave dropping as it receded, as if in sadness or
fatigue. Justin realized that he'd shouted—both of them
had shouted for help, though at the last moment somehow he had tightened the syllable to *Hey*.

You forgot your cell, didn't you? she whispered.

There'll be more cars.

They can't *hear* us, Justin. You always forget your cell! I knew it.

People'll be going by.

Not till the morning. I feel like there isn't, there won't be enough air.

Don't worry, there will.

And I *really* have to go.

She'd never sounded so much like a small girl. Or girly woman. And sometimes he'd longed for that, for a small, unshielded part of her to give itself over to his chivalry and guardianship. But this went too far. Her stomach (invisible now, though as he jabbed the LED on his watch, 1:22 a.m., he got a subaquatic glimpse of her nestled form)—her stomach had a washboard look, tanned, much harder and stronger than his own. She was crying, whimpers mixed with convulsive little intakes of breath, like a child post-tantrum. Finding her hands he held them close between their chests. The trunk seemed to be rocking slightly as if from the adrenaline thump of his pulse, their hearts together. Spending the night together after all. He'd studied murky ultrasound images of curled fetuses, and one time twins—soon to be FAS siblings—the victims of ignorant, careless or despairing parents. Entombed in their toxic primordial sea, the two had seemed to be holding each other in a consoling embrace.

Help, help, she was calling weakly.

Another car passed, slower. Again he yelled involuntarily, aware of a swelling node of panic he was compressing under his heart.

Might have let us go if you said I was claustrophobic.

Okay, Janna. He tried to speak normally. A laryngeal whisper came out. Let me think.

I mean, he won't want us to die in here! He doesn't want to go to jail for that!

You're going to be fine, Jan.

How the fuck do *you* know if I'm going to be fine! You didn't even remember I'm claustrophobic!

Janna.

You're supposed to be a doctor!

I'm not a doctor, you know that. Jesus.

You're crushing my *hands*, Justin!

Her whine seemed to split his head. This felt like the most savage hangover—worse than the worst he had undergone in university and grad school, before he met Janna and set his life on a stabler footing. A student of booze, he had been. My years of research, he would quip.

Jesus, Janna, calm down.

Why is no one walking past? Most nights I lie there and it's, it's. It's like an endless parade of people walking past. Yahoos shouting.

Someone will. Don't worry. We'll call. I—

I just *knew* you wouldn't have your cell. How can we call if—

Shut up! I mean *call*.

This just fuelled her. She wrung her hands free, panting in the tight space. No, no, you're *not* a doctor and it's lucky. You've got no—no—you can never just be *together*, can you, Justin? Why can't you just *arrange* yourself for once? It makes me crazy! You're always—

I'm telling you, enough.

Oh, your bedside manner.

Her breaths were shallow, the sour smell filling the trunk.

You're going to hyperventilate, Janna. That's the only way you won't get enough air, if you hyperventilate.

I can't help it! Get me out of here, Justin!

What are you doing?

Okay. Okay—I'm on my back, I'm pushing up with my feet. You do it too.

Janna—

Like a leg press. I'm strong. It's an old car.

Ten years isn't old for a Volvo. This came to him from somewhere—a line from some ad? His father, years ago? She was grunting, doing her press. At the fitness centre she used a personal trainer and was toying with the idea of becoming one herself. After a few seconds he rolled onto his back and tried it. It was tight, the angle too acute.

Come on, she breathed out, please please please please. Come on, come on.

The only motion, a slight flexing of the metal. Then more of that suspensioned rocking, below. A passerby might think lovers were in the back seat of the car.

I hear something, he said. He wanted to cover her panting mouth with his hand. Listen.

Oh God, it's someone. Help! she said, but with no breath in it.

Hello! he yelled, amazed at how the enclosure, and somehow the darkness too, seemed to stifle the shout. He squirmed out of his leg-press crouch as steps approached. This move involved shoving contortions, Janna crying out weakly, cursing him as his knee met her shoulder, he guessed. He didn't care now. This was the point in the old film where the hero slaps the hysterical woman and she gets a hold of herself, grateful, admiring, won over.

He got his mouth up against the crack of the trunk, near where it latched. Hello! Help!

The footsteps stopped.

In here, please! We're in the car!

The trunk, Janna whispered.

We're in the trunk!

Footsteps approached. They sounded heavy, solid. A good thing.

Someone in there?

Yes.

Yes! Janna called with a sob. Her breathing was slower, though still shallow.

What, there's two of you?

Yes.

What are you doing in there? A faint slur yoked the words together. The voice was low and throaty—older. Actually, the voice sounded a bit tickled.

We got locked in. A guy robbed us.

No way! What a fucking drag! I never seen anything like this.

Please, Janna said.

Can you just open the trunk? Justin said. The key might be in the lock there. Or maybe on the ground somewhere.

Hmm. Not in the lock.

Or just call the police. My fiancée is claustrophobic.

Yeah? The wife, she's got that too, as a matter of—

Have you got a phone?

What's that? Oh yeah, at home. Let me see if I can see a key around here.

The keychain is of, uh . . . it's Elvis, his head.

Not having much luck here. The man started to whistle softly, in tune. *It's now or never.*

I think I'm going to pee, Janna whispered.

Hold on, Justin said. Would you please hurry up, mister?

Hey, I'm doing my best for you, chief!

Maybe you should just go call the cops.

No! Janna said. The key has to be around here!

He might've just stole it, the man said. It's not on the road here.

I don't see why he would have, Justin said stubbornly, hoping the words into truth.

Why didn't he take the car? Nice car. I like these European cars.

He tried, Justin said, reaching to hold Janna's quivering shoulder. He couldn't drive standard.

A momentary silence, then the man burst out in

snorty guffaws. Oh now that's too good! he said finally. Guy couldn't drive standard!

I can't hold it, Janna said. Oh God.

It's all right, Justin whispered.

Oh *God*, get me *out* of here, *please!*

Go call the cops now, please! Justin yelled.

All right, yeah, I will so. I will now. But I was just wondering something first . . .

What?

Got nothing but shit for luck these days. Never the luck, the wife says. If you know what I'm saying. Could you give me a little retainer?

A what?

You know, a retainer. It's legal talk, like on TV. A fee. He paused and then said, firmly: Slip me out some money, whatever you got. I need it. Then I'll call the cops for you. There's a payphone up the street.

I told you, we were just robbed!

Justin, wait.

We don't have a cent. How the fuck can you ask—

Justin!

Now hang on a minute, chief—I told you, I'm broke, and I'm going to be doing you a favour. I mean, I prefer not to have anything to *do* with cops if it's up to myself. This is going out on a limb for me. It's not like you can't afford it. Look at this car. This fucking *Volvo*.

But we—

It's okay, Janna said, I have something. Some money.

What? Justin said.

Just slip whatever you got through the crack, here by the latch. I can pry, maybe. I got some keys here.

My keys, Justin said. Janna, what are you—

I always keep a twenty separate, she said, in case.

Of course, Justin whispered.

What?

Of course you do, he told her, and now in his mind he saw, not with doting amusement but a stressed rage, Janna opening doors with her hooked pinkie, or with the same fey digit keying in her PIN at the automatic teller. This although, he'd explained, on any given day a person encountered a dozen infectious agents which, if you were weakened enough, could make you ill or worse. But she was strong—probably all the more so for her years of working with the public at the bistro, where she also did the pinkie thing. Where it must be seen as a stylish or campy affectation, not another symptom of her leery, meticulous nature.

A twenty is good, the man said. Try to slip it through here.

No! Justin said. Put the money away, Janna. He was groping in the dark, flashing the LED, trying to find her hand.

Justin, for God's sake, I'm going to get us out of here. Someone has to.

Let her give me the money, asshole. The voice was closer now, the man kneeling, it seemed. I think you can slip it out here.

How do we know you'll even help us, Justin said, if we give you the money?

It's like you got a choice here? The voice was sneering. Justin inhaled sharply. Then the man added, *Duh!*—and this, for Justin, was the end. This soft little *duh*.

Fuck you! You can take our keys and your phone call and your—shove them up your ass, if you know how to find it. And I'm going to find you tomorrow! The cops are going to—

A horrific slamming beat down on them from above, then it seemed to emanate from all directions, a pummelling they felt inside, slower and steadier than their bolting hearts, as the man hammered the trunk with a fist or the flat of his hand. It could have been a street gang smashing the car with tire irons, bats. Justin rushed his hands to his ears and then to Janna's ears, to protect what was left of her nerves. Stop! he cried. The slamming went on, Janna making a steady high whine of pain or terror. He tried pushing up on the trunk with his fist to absorb the vibrations. He rammed his palm upward once, a feeble counterblow the man nevertheless must have felt, because now he whacked the metal harder and faster. Justin curled on the floor of the trunk, clamping his palms over Janna's ears, then over his own, back and forth. Though their bodies were jammed together at many points, in this extremity he was fully alone. She must feel the same. He guessed she must feel the same. The beating ended. Heavy footsteps stalked away. The night was quiet again. She was breathing slower—small, sobby catches of breath coming at longer intervals. There was a smell like ammonia and he thought he felt dampness through the right knee of his jeans. He rested a hand on her hip. She seemed to be drifting into a kind of sleep, or a gradual faint, her nervous system, he guessed, no longer able to take the stress.

Now that he didn't have a conscious Janna to coax along, the full weight of his own fear and anger returned. He sobbed for a moment, no tears, eyelids clamped on dryness. Not for the first time he wondered if they actually could suffocate in here. Maybe that was why she'd lost consciousness. His breathing felt tight, but that could just be fear. The trauma of his head blow. A car passed, then another, and he made no effort to cry out.

After a time, soft footsteps approached.

Hello! Please help us! He tried to shout gently, afraid of ripping Janna from her stupor.

Is someone in there? A soft tone, a sort of eunuch voice—the vocal equivalent of the footsteps. Justin explained things, trying to sound calm, murmuring through the crack through which he felt, just once, a cool breath of air. The man listened with a few faint sounds of encouragement. He seemed to be kneeling close to Justin's mouth. The man was an orderly, he said, on the way to the hospital to start his shift on the maternity ward. It was almost five a.m. He would flag down the first car he saw, he said, and get somebody to phone the police, or he would find a payphone, or call from the hospital if all else failed. That would be ten minutes from now. He would run. The odd, adenoidal voice trailed off, and soft steps—rubber-soled, Justin guessed—jogged away into the night.

Justin left his head against the cool of the metal, his mouth as near as possible to the crack from which that one clean breath of air had seemed to seep. As another draft reached him, tears surged into his eyes with a wide-angle shot of great vapourless skies and fenceless emerald meadows . . . like a tourist still of the prairies, although he could *smell* the fields. There would be air enough, at least. The police would come soon.

Surely, whatever happened, they would live differently now.

A car was nearing slowly. It cruised past. Perhaps the police, searching for the Volvo they had been told to look for. But the car didn't double back. Another passed, then another. The sparse traffic of early dawn. It was 5:12. In the eerie light of his watch, her sleeping face was peaceful except for the abiding crease between her eyes. Now she was nestled hard against him in the cold, his arm tight around her, his hand splayed wide on her back to cover as much of her as he could. Were old married couples ever buried in the same coffin? he wondered. He had never heard of it, but surely it happened. Or was there some law against it? Another half-hour passed and the little pre-dawn rush hour seemed to end. Why was he not mystified, or at least puzzled, by this

latest lack of help, or by its slowness? He felt just numb.
There was never any telling. Now and then other cars
came from the west or from the east, but none slowed
or stopped. Real help would come eventually, of
course—the sidewalks would soon be thronged. Another
hour or two. Three at most. What was another hour
or two in a lifetime together?

———

A curious thing he noticed in the years after: in company, he and Janna would often discuss that night,
either collaborating to broach the story on some apt
conversational cue (which they would both recognize
without having to exchange a glance), or readily indulg-
ing a request from guests, or hosts, to hear it for the
first time, or yet again. And even when passing through
a troubled spell in their marriage, they would speak of
each other's actions that night only in proud, approving
ways. Janna with her granite will, he would say, had
faced a claustrophobic's worst nightmare and remained
the more rational of them throughout. *She'd probably
have got us out of there hours earlier if I'd just listened.*
Justin, she would insist, had been competent and forceful the way she had always wanted him to be and had
kept her from totally "losing it." Justin would then pro-
fess chagrin at how he himself had lost it, screaming at
their potential saviour, though in fact he was partial to
the memory of that recklessly manly tantrum—and on
Janna's face, as she watched him replay the scene, a

suspended half-smile would appear, a look of fond exasperation. But when the story was done and they left to drive home, or their guests did, a silence would settle between them—not a cold or embarrassed silence, but a pensive, accepting one—and they would say nothing more of that night or its latest rendition. When they were alone together, in fact, they never spoke a word of it.

[OUTTRIP]

Late afternoon, your third day in the desert, the Fisher catches up with you. You're not sure why he's called the Fisher and you've never had the balls to ask him. According to one story, he got the alias a few years ago, back home, after the period when a number of cats and small dogs turned up dead and mutilated, and for a while people in the Heights guessed they were the victims of some psycho. It turned out they were killed by a fisher—a kind of large, nocturnal weasel—that had come down out of the woods along the Cataraqui.

Maybe too the nickname stuck because it sounds a bit like "pusher."

When the Fisher comes walking toward you up the dry streambed, tracing the path your own boots have left in the dirt, you are not surprised. In fact you

have the feeling you've *summoned* him here, though
even now—after three days alone in the wilds above
Osoyoos in a heat wave, parched and hungry—you're
sufficiently self-aware to wonder if it's really him.
Really anyone at all.

It was not supposed to be this hot, even here, in
mid-July, but the Program doesn't cancel its "client"
OutTrips. Rain or shine. (You've never seen rain here.)
Your first OutTrip was three days, in June. Afternoons
on the desert floor were smelter hot and after midnight
you shivered in your thermal blanket. Still, there was
never a moment when you feared you wouldn't make
it out alive. This five-day trip—the climax of the
Program, after which you'll debrief and fly east to face
a few months' probation and then, supposedly, get on
with your life—is different. Though you're way, way
fitter and tougher now than when you arrived sick and
skinny at the camp, you've been struggling. By the end
of day 2 you were struggling. The "staple quotient" of
water was challenge enough on OutTrip 1. This time
you guess it's dangerous. If it gets too hot, travel at
night and sleep through the day—that was the instruc-
tion, and starting tonight you mean to follow it.

It's around five p.m., you guess, and with hours to
go until dusk you're resting in the louvered shade of a
stand of stunted firs. You can see down the streambed
to the valley, a full day's walk away, where irrigated
vineyards roll greenly to a cool blue lake: a small,
V-shaped vision of the promised land. Not even a

breath of breeze. Sweat pearls on your face and trickles from your armpits to the waistband of your boxer shorts; as if you can afford to lose fluid. In the silence you think you hear the needles of the firs drying up and falling onto the dead ones with the sub-audible ticking that ice crystals make as they form from your breath and fall on the coldest winter nights, back east.

You keep dreaming of such cold.

You plan to walk by the light of the moon—not much of a moon these nights, but it'll have to do—using your map and compass. The next cache of water and food is fifteen kilometres from here. All you want is the water. In this ragged terrain it'll take you until five or six in the morning, just after sunrise.

What are you doing here? you ask, your voice hoarse and corroded.

Serious efforts were required to locate you, the Fisher says as he slows and stops, spotlit by the sun behind you and this puny, pathetic brake of firs. He looks unfazed by the incinerating heat. He has on black sport loafers, designer jeans manufactured to look worn and ripped, and a form-fitting, large-collared yellow shirt he wears open to the third button and tucked stringently into his jeans. He's older, maybe forty, but that doesn't fully explain the tight tuck; a lot of guys his age dress loosely, like teenagers. He seems to model his look on porn stars of the '80s—a compact, gelled helmet of ginger hair, ample sideburns, aviator shades with red lenses that allow just the slightest glimpse of the eyes behind. He wears a black belt, thick, an ostentatious silver buckle. The gold Rolex is likely real.

He looks down at you speculatively. Slowly he bares those even teeth with the large, jeering gap between the front incisors. It's a smile that always enjoys itself a little too much. A coarse smile, a cannibal's wide rictus; every time he smiles, he belies his pretensions to refinement.

You ran, Ben, even though I told you Upper Mongolia wouldn't be far enough. (A classic Fisherism. He sees himself as a superior being, a polymath, and in fact he knows a great deal about many things, but his information is all a few degrees off, as if his brain makes slight data-entry errors with the info he probably gleans from dicey blogs and websites. It's the same with his extensive but wonky diction.)

I'm not running, you say, holding your voice in place as it tries to slip up the register, thin out and vanish.

You don't look like you can even walk now, Ben.

Are you going to sit? I'm afraid I can't offer you anything. I have to hike from meal to meal here. Drink to drink.

Sure, I grasp completely how the Program operates.

Of course you do! you insist, as if to convince yourself: the Fisher cannot be here in front of you, even if all the details are right, including the voice that he always slows down and gruffens, like Donald Rumsfeld. You're just me! This isn't for real—I'm dreaming you.

He takes another step toward you and nimbly folds downward, without the aid of his arms, assuming a

loose lotus position. He always moves with this easy
aplomb—a Zen abbot's serene poise crossed with a
pimp's air of dignity. A self-pampered, theatrical dignity. But he does feel the heat: perspiration glazes his
tanned, lined face, sequins of sweat dot his auburn chest
curls. There are stains around his armpits and you smell
deodorant—his usual perfumy brand, incongruously
feminine. Over his shoulder the far valley of vineyards
wavers in convected heat as the sun sears these arid
slopes like the surface of Mercury. The rocks are about
to crack, like clay in a kiln.

Your father, a Baptist minister, left your mother and
you in Kingston ten years ago and started a second
family out west while founding his own church, or cult,
as the Saskatchewan RCMP now call it. He's rich, his
acolytes give him everything they have, and he's paying
for your stay out here. He has not seen you or your
mother since he left. The money he sends—not a lot—
is conditional on this continuing estrangement. His
commune is based in the Palliser Triangle, a near-desert
about a thousand kilometres due east of here. You could
walk there in a month of nights.

You hear yourself ask, Got any water?

I thought you concluded I was some kind of . . .
figment.

Where's Vladimir, then? you ask, knowing the Fisher
goes nowhere without him. Vladimir is a stately but
stunned-looking borzoi that some folks assume the
Fisher must sedate, for reasons of his own. All of the

Fisher's reasons are his own. You suppose that's one definition of freedom.

Oh, come on, Ben, you know what it's like flying long-haul with a dog. They have to travel caged up in the fuselage.

Hold, you mumble.

What's that? Ah—correct. It is cold in there. And *dark*. No food or water. It's sickening to think of the atrocities people afflict on animals. And now you know how it feels to need water.

No, I meant "hold" as opposed to "fuselage."

What?

Nothing.

You owe me a fuck of a wad, Benjamin.

I have nothing to *do* with you anymore. You're not even here! I'm asleep, or delirious, or something. Fuck, maybe I'm dying . . .

Let's not get ahead of ourselves, Ben.

Do you have any . . . you don't have any water?

Correct and incorrect.

You actually lean toward him, though for the last few minutes you've been edging away—edging away without feeling yourself move, your spine now clamped against the trunk of a fir. Its bark pricks and itches through your damp T-shirt, which you would remove if you had the energy. You say, What do you mean, *"correct and incorrect"*? If you have any . . .

(There it is again—that stretchy grin unscabbarding those teeth.)

I have just enough water so you can mix up what I brought you.

What? You brought me oxy?

You have the vague sense—the opposite of déjà vu—that you know in advance what he's going to say. As if he's a speaker in your own lucid dream. This whole scene is a kind of neurological confidence trick, your own brain the trickster. Still, you can't restrain a terrified, credulous excitement.

I've even pre-powdered them, the Fisher says. They keep making that harder to do. I don't let that stop me, though. I don't want anything to stand between me and a customer, Ben—even one who no longer has a triple-A debit rating.

Credit rating, you think. I don't owe you anything, you say in your dried-up voice. You took everything! Three years, maybe a hundred thousand bucks, my fucking freedom, my peace of mind. I owe all sorts of people money, but you I owe nothing.

Ah, Ben. You're like everyone else. You believe that due to my not assuming an official business, I don't retain scrupulous accounts.

No, I'm sure you do.

And your attitude, Ben—frankly it's a disappointment, not to mention a forcible kick in the balls. You think I usually jet across the country to resupply clients like this?

The thermals rising off the rocks and sand of the gully floor behind the Fisher now seem to rise *out* of him, like steam above an angry cartoon figure. Figure, figment, phantom. You scrunch your eyes closed and feel the dryness in the corners and between the eyeball and lid, an itching, gritty distress like a corneal abrasion. The body is a machine that, like any other, breaks down if the lubricants run out. You open your eyes: he's still there, looking down at the sunglasses he now holds in his hand. The reason his glasses sit a bit crookedly on his face is that a chunk is missing from the top of his right ear—deducted by a switchblade or a bullet, according to rumour.

His black eyes swivel upward and meet yours. Your breathing stalls. The whites of his eyes are very white, healthy-looking, though the skin below is puffy and discoloured. It's a rare view. Seeing at intimate range those contused pouches, it hits you that he constantly wears the sunglasses not so much for purposes of intimidation as out of vanity.

What do you want from me? I've got nothing here. We *carry* nothing out here—no money, nothing. I don't even have a watch. And it's not like I have hundreds of bucks back at the camp, either.

Hundreds wouldn't begin to cover it, Ben. Aren't you a little old for a juvie boot camp?

There are a bunch of guys in their twenties. It was a condition of my sentence.

I told you, I'm fully cognizant of all that.

Of course you are. You're in my mind.

Ben, I'm losing patience—though I have to say this

is an original gambit. No client has ever tried to infer I was a vision, or a demon. Brilliant, Ben. Of course I know you have no money on you. But your debt, honestly, your debt is only one aspect of the issue. You see, in a way I'm *sentimental* about my customers, Ben. They're like . . . extended family. I don't have a family to speak of, you see. Besides Vlad.

You? Sentimental?

A weakness, I know.

He glances down and slips the red sunglasses back on.

I liked having you as a customer, Ben. I valued that special relationship we had and to tell you the truth I still do, even though you've abused my credibility. I can forgive that. I committed mistakes when I was your age. I can even forgive that you referenced me to the authorities, Ben—the fucking *authorities*. Men with no *class*. But I expect our special relationship to continue after you come home.

I'm clean now. Just leave me alone.

Honestly, Ben, it's more about . . . about principle than money.

Why aren't you locked up? you croak. Why am *I* the one who ends up hallucinating in the desert and on fucking probation?

It's not like I haven't done time, Ben. But it was the making of me. I grew very focused in there. I read expansively and learned to meditate. I quit smoking and I had to quit drinking and I started to keep fit—maybe a bit like this boot camp of yours. I now eat a Neolithic diet: no refined flour or sugar, minimal meat, lots of nuts, seeds and beans. And lentils, Ben—lentils are an excellent food.

If you're not just me dreaming, then prove it. Tell me something I don't know.

Ah, but Ben, you know plenty of stuff you don't *know* you know, so what kind of proof would that be?

I don't know what the temperature was yesterday in Kingston. Cool, I bet, down by the boatyards. God—cool and with a lake breeze! Tell me what the temperature was.

I can do better, Ben. He proffers his clenched hand as if for a fist bump. I dislike when people touch me, Ben—honestly, I *hate* it, hate it with a serious aversion—but if it would help you to believe, go ahead.

On the back of the hand, a pelt of carrot-coloured hair.

Ben?

No, you say, I'm good.

Delirium, psychosis, either is preferable to being trapped out here with the real Fisher, hours from help, in the remote northern spur of a desert that goes on forever, a hundred days' hike south across the U.S. border and the western states, deep into Mexico. The Greater Sonoran Desert. Till now, it's been your new favourite place in the world and these OutTrips your favourite activity. For the first time in years, something other than substance abuse has rallied your full attention, subdued the pathological patter in your brain—your exceptional brain, according to certain tests that "experts" at the university gave you a year after your father deserted his family and small Kingston flock. Not something you've ever felt proud of, this IQ. More like burdened, ashamed—something to conceal if you live in the Heights. Your brain's babble, the second-guessing, self-accusing, the standing outside your life, watching and thinking, thinking, always *thinking*, never eased, not until the opiates, especially oxycodone. That neural noise was just your big fat brain trying to fill the silence of the badlands inside you, the way a lost man might yell and mutter to himself because the quiet of the wilderness—the sound of his coming demise—is too awful.

Being out here has changed everything. Your inner badlands have found their match and now inner and outer worlds conform, void to void—a strangely consoling balance. You're no freak after all. Your inner state (now wonderfully quiet!) reflects the world's quantum vacancy. The Buddha's vision of formlessness and freedom was right, your father wrong (his sect is based on the notion that *everyone* is possessed, either by Christ or the Antichrist).

There was a breeze off the lake, Ben. Pleasant weather. You'll be a lot happier when you come back. Wait, where do you think you're going, we're not finished here!

I'm heading on to the next cache.

You're in no condition.

Actually I'm in great condition for the first time in my life, and I can do it. You, on the other hand, are going to start feeling the heat and the terrain and you'll fall behind.

Even if I'm just figmentary, Ben? (Out come those terrifying teeth.)

You heft your daypack and turn and walk off through the little screen of firs and emerge on a ridge that gives a wide-angle view down into another, shallower valley. Another range of bare hills on the far side. The vast mural of the sky is cloudless, blue as the marrow of a paraffin flame. The Fisher can't be real and if the Fisher *is* real he will soon collapse; he leads a pimp-slash-pusher's pampered life, while you—you've survived on the street for years, only rarely shuffling the three klicks home to the wartime bungalow of your mother. She is shattered, sick with fear, the true victim of the piece. Your own victim, partly. You're out here to change everything, to return whole and help her. Just loving her again will help her. True addicts can't love. The addiction conscripts all the love in them and degrades it, shits it out as something used and useless.

This valley looks barren, devoid of vineyards and the other postcard features of the main valley behind you—long lakes, clusters of condos, sun-white wineries like prosperous haciendas. But a shimmering thread runs along the valley floor and you think: stream.

The Fisher's footfalls crunch behind you.

I'd like you to stop, Ben. You know I can detain you if necessary. I'm being restrained so far in not doing so.

Maybe if you walk far enough, drain yourself utterly, your brain will no longer be able to project these fantasies; like a director and film crew whose budget is exhausted. You say, We're continuing north through this valley, onto that far ridge. Then west along the ridge-line. Maybe an hour.

I'm happy to hear you including me now, Ben. But you should reconsider this trek. You're not walking normally.

Blisters.

Remember, when the pain gets too much, I'm there— I can help! Slow down, Ben, it's steep here, you'll twist an ankle. Were you aware that climbers get seriously injured more often on *downhill* stretches? Radical strains in the femoral ligaments. Benjamin? Slow down!

The voice is losing ground. You're outrunning your delirium. *Just get yourself down into that valley.* The shade deepening there, that glimmering seam of water.

All right, Ben, I see you're determined to get down there. Fair enough. I'll go with you. I concur the view is spectacular on this side.

You're panting the dry air, sauna-hot in your nostrils and throat. Your lungs, parched as the rest of you, have lost the ability to moisturize air. Your insides are desert-ifying. Your legs wobble as if you've just had casts removed and the muscles are wasted. Preliminary chills now, nausea—those early symptoms of heatstroke they

warned you about in camp. And now a terrible thought
rears up: what if the Fisher is following you to drive you
on to exhaustion and death? What makes the thought
so awful is that if the Fisher is a chimera—and he must
be: he can't be real—then really it's just *you* goading
yourself toward death. This wouldn't be the first time
in your life you've tried to die, but over the last few
weeks you feel you have surmounted such desperation,
finally and fully. You glance back. The Fisher has almost
caught up. He nods genially. If he were wearing a hat,
he'd be tipping the brim. The thing about aviator shades,
you realize, is the lenses are shaped like the eye sockets
of a skull.

His left hand on your shoulder: that gold band like
a wedding ring, though it's on the middle finger.

How could you let the authorities *catch* you, Ben? He
pauses for breath. I thought you'd developed some pro-
ficiency. They say if you succeed in stealing a hundred
times, you'll go on forever without apprehension.

You know how it happened. You know everything I
know.

I'd appreciate hearing your personal recount. His
hand tightens on your shoulder. In fact, Ben, I insist.

You wrench your shoulder free, run staggeringly
downhill. There is no trail. A trail isn't needed. The
ground is bare but for thatches of dry, tough scrub that
you deke around in a clumsy, desperate slalom, your
quads hammered and weakening. Your ears pop with
the descent and your daypack jounces against your

sunburned shoulders. You're descending so quickly, you fast-track the sun's setting behind the deep valley's far side, that ripsaw ridgeline. The valley bottom is out of focus but surging up toward you, a trickle of cool creek, the oasis shade of trees.

You can no longer hear the Fisher's footsteps.

The valley floor *is* shaded, cool—the sun occluded by that far ridge—but it's parched. You stand in a white streambed of chalk or limestone cracked and sinkholed here and there, weeds sprouting, like the remains of an ancient road in the Holy Land. You travelled there with your father and mother about a year before he left; everywhere you went, he had his bifocalled nose in a guidebook or a map or his Bible, raging at you or your mother if you interrupted him. . . . When you looked down from the ridge a quarter-hour ago, this streambed must have reflected the sun like water. To either side of it, sagebrush and a few small, knurled thorn trees languish. You sag onto the polished stone that still holds the sun's warmth, lick the sweat off your biceps and forearms, then tug off your T-shirt and chew on the fabric, trying to suck in the moisture. You look back up the valley's side. Nothing. You've shaken up or deprived your brain enough that the lucid delirium has passed. Now think. You need to rest in the shade, unmoving, till the temperature drops and you can climb the far ridge and follow it to the next cache. Saint-Exupéry, after crashing his small plane, walked for days—no, nights—in the Sahara without water.

A sound from upstream and your eyes startle toward it. A scuttling in that thicket of greasewood a hundred metres off—something under the lower twigs. A tail like a puff of smoke seems to plume and vanish.

Another mirage.

You're base-jumping down through space into star-fields and vast nebular clusters—you waken to vertigo, which eases, leaving you splayed in the streambed staring up at the sky. To the Syilx peoples of this high desert, the Milky Way was the Road of Souls. From beyond the ridge that you staggered down—a black, brooding absence of stars and planets on one side of your planetarium—the moon's light is crowning. You're shivering with cold and your open mouth is utterly dry as if, while you slept, one of those dental spit siphons has been functioning. In jail you saw a dentist for the first time in years. He said you were lucky to have any teeth left in your mouth, and *good* teeth, too. He must have assumed it was crystal meth that drove you to crime, though you were never drawn to meth, which would only have accelerated your hyperactive left hemisphere.

You sit up and again there's motion upstream. A faint sound, too, a trickling, as if you're in a motel and someone in the next room has left a tap running. From your daypack you take the thermal hoodie the Program supplied (penitentiary orange, not merely to discourage clients from fleeing the Program, but also to encourage local ranchers and townsfolk to report escapees and even rustle them back to camp, for a two-hundred-dollar reward). You pull on the hoodie and crawl up the streambed toward the sound. The Road of Souls so densely radiant, your head casts a weak shadow. You totter to your feet, grope onward. A horn of the moon jabs over the ridgeline. The sound from ahead grows clearer. Water. A delusion, it must be, but there's no way you can stop. The moon is suddenly up over the ridgeline, glazing the valley in feeble light—a muted, lunar fax of the sun's light, but enough to bring out two eyes beading in the thicket of greasewood ahead. Your heart thumps its way up your gullet into your mouth. The eyes are gone. The Program does not allow flashlights. The Program's purpose is to drop you near naked into the wilderness so you'll find out what's left of you when every accessory is stripped away. An infant, unaccommodated, with the chance to start over. Born again and all that. There is something of the religious cult in the Program. Still, for the most part it works—though you gather there have been a few deaths and suicides over the years.

There's a deeper darkness beyond the greasewood, and the trickling sound is coming from there. Your brain, animating all this (you're certain that's what's happening), seems determined to frighten you to death. You can't go in there without a flashlight and yet you have to, you have to find out if there really is water dripping deliciously in that cave—it must be a cave. It's not a cave, you see as you approach, it's the mouth of an old mine. You reach up to touch the punky, hammocked lintel over the opening. A rank smell wafts out, as if foxes have denned inside. Bats, maybe. Along with the stink there's a cool, humid quality to the air. You duck your head and enter, groping at the dark, inching your feet along the floor that slopes downward slightly, could fall away steeply, a mineshaft. You shuffle on toward the liquid sound. You're beyond the penumbral light of the threshold, maybe thirty steps in: dense darkness. You glance back for the anchoring assurance of moonlight and starlight framed in the mine's mouth and a silhouette slips across it, leaving the mine or entering. You stand rigid, water audible on one side of you, the glowing square of the mine's mouth on the other.

Who is it? you call.

From somewhere in the mine, a deep thoracic rumbling, like a big creature's warning growl. The roots of the hair on your nape prickle and freeze.

Fuck off! you say. I don't fucking *believe* in you!

The flick of a match sharp as a gunshot. You spin around, toward the trickling. The Fisher—his face lamped by the flame he holds near his chin—sits by a greenish patch of polished rock where water drips out of a hole and flows down the wall, vanishing into a crevice between wall and floor. He holds the shrinking match until its flame seems to transfer to the tips of his thumb and index finger, which he then shakes, plunging the mine into a darkness deeper than before.

What do you suppose they mined here? he asks.

You're the one who thinks he knows everything, you whisper; a whisper is all you have left.

I'm surmising coal, he says. Anthracite. Though I suppose it could have been something more valuable. Even gold. Either way, a hell of a lot of effort for what it must have paid.

You've found a better way.

Correct, Ben. But don't be so quick to judge.

Who better than me?

Do you believe in God, Ben? Do you believe in anything beyond this, um . . .

You're going to tell me to leave judgment to God, right? That's what my father used to say. (You're torn, desperate for that water but afraid to approach.)

Ben, a superior being can perceive things that you can't. That's his *avocation*. If you could see with such a being's—

What I see is that if He exists, He's on the side of the strong.

Ah, the spiritually strong! The Gandhis and the Dalai Lamas, right, Ben?

The opposite. The despots and the sharks. The Ponzis and the chairmen, the pontiffs, colonels, the white-collar crooks. And ones like you—God's on your side, Fisher. That's why the ones like you thrive and the softer ones end up in slums or asylums or cancer wards. The meek—the meek inherit the halfway house, or—

Benjamin—

Or the detox ward.

Benjamin, sit down and rest, have a drink, have a little sniff, you sound *awful*.

I'm not one of those anymore.

That's excellent, Ben—that's very, very good! Do you understand why? Because if you're not one of them, then before long—not yet, but soon—you'll be one of *us*.

Forget it.

But you're *smart*, Ben, so you understand that you have to be one or the other. The nice ones, they think they're harmless, herbivorous, injuring no one. The honest ones know it's all about finding a place on the food chain and acknowledging your niche. (He pronounces it *nitch*.) You can't live and thrive without hurting others, Ben. Me, if I do hurt anyone, I hurt the weak-willed and—present company exclusive—the *stupid*, which is much preferred to harming the intelligent and the strong, the way some persons do. I fit into the Darwinian diorama, Ben. I'm simply culling the flock.

You move toward the water, squat down, reach out. You hear the Fisher's breathing pause and change as he rises to his feet so that your positions are reversed: he now stands over you.

Ben . . . I can't let you share this good water until I have your word.

I'm through with you. Leave me alone.

As you reach toward the wall, as you smell and feel your way toward that luscious, humid coolness, his hand grips your wrist. A painfully tight clasp.

I cull the flock, Benjamin, but I also provide a *service*. The termination of all pain, Ben. Pain like this! I make it all go away. And Ben, you *are* weak. You know it. You still need me and you know it.

Let go of me! You try to grab his hand but now he clutches the wrist of your free hand and he's pushing both wrists downward, forcing you toward the floor of the mine. You whiplash your lowered head backward to wrench free and hear the stony thunk before you feel it—the top of your skull has clouted some hard thing and it can't be the roof of the mine, you're too low, and now the Fisher's guttural moan sirens into a howl of pain and you know you've butted him in the chin or nose. His grip loosens on both wrists. You twist free and scramble toward the mine's glowing mouth. In your panic to get away you're actually fleeing the precious water. You hear him, his flat steps heavy, implacable as pursuing feet in a nightmare, which is what this is, you tell yourself again, and the telling flits like an urgent news update along the base of a screen, impossible to hold in mind. You emerge into the night and the deep valley seems brilliant as morning, somehow the moon now straight overhead and the stars reeling in counterintuitive constellations, and again you see darting motion behind the scrub to your left: three creatures, coywolves, their eyes glowing redly as in a botched photo, teeth bared, and they too must be apparitions, but by the time they've sprung and brought down the Fisher as he emerges, you've forgotten you're dreaming, if you are, and the Fisher's cries—*help me, fuck, help me, Ben, please!*—resonate through the valley, each syllable in its slow dying as sweet as the trickle of water from a deep, sulphurless, cave-cool spring. Drink now and be revived.

[THE DEAD ARE MORE VISIBLE]

A graveyard shift meant time-and-a-half but she would have worked these January nights, flooding the park rinks, for regular pay. She worked alone and liked the peace of it. In the small office attached to the skaters' warming hut, she kept a Thermos of heavily sweetened coffee, her new radio/CD player, a few magazines and a horror or romance novel, neatly packing and taking them home in a duffel bag when her shift ended in the morning dark. Friends would ask if it didn't get lonely. Sure, at times, but if you have to be alone at night anyway, you might as well be working, earning time-and-a-half, instead of alone in the bed.

And working alone saved fuss—dealing with bosses, or with co-workers who always had a grievance to share and wanted you to take their view. Ellen got along fine with them, but they often vexed each other, and who needed to be around that? She'd always found it natural to get along with people. She didn't understand the general crankiness of the world. Often now it seemed easier, if not exactly preferable, to be alone. In earlier jobs she'd had bosses peering over her shoulder all the time—often touching her shoulder, in fact. That groping had died out some years ago and she didn't miss those confidential hands, though she did sometimes miss the looks, all the candid, famished stares that had helped define her teen years and early twenties. Still, she'd never found it as hard to be alone as some of her friends claimed it was. If you got along well with people, you got along with yourself. She believed that as a general rule. In a sense, she was well made for this stage of her life. Look at it that way.

After her first hour or so, flooding the shinny rink and the children's oval, she would come back into the office to warm up while the ice set. She would unzip the front of her black snowmobile suit and slip her feet out of the big Sorels and prop back in the conference chair by the space heater, sipping coffee and reading. Tonight it was *The Shell Seekers* and she would read a good half of its 582 pages before dawn. Harlequins had bored her for some years. No substance, no surprise. They kept you company for an hour or so and then evaporated, leaving no trace. As for horror novels— these freezing nights, nobody around, were just made for them. She liked Thomas Harris and H.P. Lovecraft and lately she'd been rereading early Stephen King.

Depending on the night's coldness, after an hour or two of reading under the lone fluorescent tube she would turn the water back on and pull on her wool gloves and, over them, a pair of industrial rubber gloves, then go out for another round of flooding. Her third or fourth round, near dawn, would finish the night. It took at least three really cold nights to get the rinks up and running in each park, and then there was plenty of maintenance, night and day, after that. This park, unofficially Skeleton Park (it had been the city's main cemetery through the 1800s), was her favourite. She liked its office, preferring the fire-like, toasting heat of the space heater to the electric baseboards in the other, larger offices. And this was pretty much the part of town where she'd grown up. It was changing, of course. Students and young professional types were moving in, renovating the old rental properties enclosing the park on four sides—the handsome Victorian redbricks that gave the park a sort of phony, respectable frame, since just beyond were hundreds of smaller places on narrow yardless streets, much aluminum siding, low apartment blocks of bile-yellow brick. She was raised in one of those smaller houses and had skated here as a child forty years ago.

Technically she still had a boss, but out here she never had to deal with him. Not that he gave her a hard time. They got along. He was a short, fit, swaggery man of about thirty who once had a tryout with an NHL team, she could never remember which one. He treated her like one of the guys to the point of using "man"— while not exactly *calling* her "man"—when speaking to her. *Sure thing, man. Man, I wish I could tell you. You want Skeleton Park this winter, man, it's all yours.* Maybe he preferred to think that anyone so much bigger than himself, and possibly stronger, must be a sort of man. Ellen was not only sturdy—her ex-husband's back-handed compliment—but tall. She came from a side of town where most women thickened dramatically in their thirties and before long outweighed their men. The men thinned to sinew, their faces got a wrinkled, redly scoured look as if the skin had been worked with sandpaper, their eyes grew raw and haunted. Ellen had been spared the puffy moon face of her older sisters, only to see her features grow meaty and masculine while her body consolidated, almost doubling itself, like a hard-working farm wife of another era.

Her husband had left, seven years ago. No children. Gavin had never wanted any and now she supposed, accepted, that it was too late. She was forty-six and she no longer registered on men. The many she worked with—almost all of the city's outdoor and maintenance staff were men—were genial and respectful and she never felt so invisible as when they were around: robust, vital men, and they addressed her like a buddy. Or talked about women in her hearing. Maintaining the rink during the day, seeing the boys play shinny or smaller children chug around the oval in their wobbling circuits while the mothers sat watching, cheering—that could get to her too, of course. Being here at night was better, all in all.

The last few nights she wasn't even alone. On the far side of the low-boarded shinny rink, a man was standing motionless under a lamppost by the icy asphalt path. He'd been standing there for three nights. His back to the rink, he was facing the twenty-five-foot-high limestone obelisk that dominated this end of the park. He was not dressed for the activity. He wore a baseball cap and a short brown leather jacket, blue jeans, construction boots. It was about fifteen degrees below zero. He'd spoken to Ellen during the first night's flooding, while she worked the northwest corner of the rink—close enough for them to talk with slightly raised voices. She'd been waving the hose head back and forth, layering water over deepening ice. Now and then he would take a step or two toward the obelisk, pause, then resume his stiff stance. He seemed to be sighting on the thing. Later, a few steps back, a step to the side. She watched out of the corner of her eye, not especially concerned. The park was known for odd spectacles. It was a sort of open-air hostel for addicts, parolees, halfway house residents, psych hospital outpatients, a shifting population of mainly harmless eccentrics.

He'd veered his head and looked at her over his shoulder, fast, a pitcher checking a runner at first base. The visor of his cap kept his face in shadow but she could see his beard, light-coloured, neatly trimmed. He had good shoulders, a nice build.

"Have you ever seen a miracle?" he asked.

Here we go, she thought tolerantly. Then, in a cordial tone, more or less the tone she used to broach any conversation: "It all depends what you mean. You warm enough out here?"

"It has to be moved," he said. His voice was mild, reasonable.

"What, the obelisk there?"

"It's a tombstone. They resent that it's here. It weighs down the dead."

"You been talking to them?"

His head tilted slyly. "Let's just say that I have heard from them. There are twenty-four thousand of them."

"It doesn't seem possible, does it?" she said. "In a space this size. Thirty thousand was the figure I heard."

"The dead are more visible than we are. They have a legal right to this ground. There are twenty-four thousand of them. They resent that tombstone. It's undemocratic."

She'd first read the plaque on the obelisk as a child, in the '60s. Parishioners had built it with local limestone in 1826 to commemorate the loss of their minister, who had died "in the thirtieth year of his age." In Ellen's girlhood and teenage years the thing had been just another neighbourhood feature, something to throw snowballs at (two points if you hit the point of the top spire, one if you hit the stone orb below it), joke about (the more or less phallic shape, the word "erected" on the plaque), or climb on (every few years somebody fell off the upper pediment and broke an arm or got a concussion). Now she guessed she could see what the man was talking about—all the headstones were long gone, pulled from the earth like broken teeth over a century ago, while this monument to one man still towered over the park and its invisibly crammed, stacked dead.

"I can move items with my mind," the man said. "I do it at the kitchen table. If I stare hard enough, I can move this tombstone. I will need to get the angle correct. It's weighing down the dead. Once I move it, I will then dissolve it. I dissolve items."

"Couldn't you dissolve something else?" She amplified her tone of banter to get through to him. "The Revenue Canada building? Kingston Pen? This park takes a lot of hits."

His face was dark under the cap. "The dead want this tombstone moved and dissolved," he said. "This is not what I would choose to do with my evening."

"Sure is a cold one," she said.

For some moments he stared at her.

"Well, good luck to you," she told him. "I mean, I can see your point. I'll have to head across now. Stay warm now." She tugged some slack into the hose and began to slide-step over to the far boards, skirting the freshly soaked places.

"And I can tell," he called out to her back, "if someone is a good person! I look at them and I know their life!"

She turned to him with a grin—who could resist such an offer? If it was an offer.

"So then, what am I?"

She met his intent, eyeless stare. She'd never, even lonely or hurt, found it hard to meet a stare. She bore no guilt.

"You are a good person."

She smiled again. "Thank you. You stay warm."

Third night of flooding, two a.m. Plenty of work in the corners and along the boards, where the ice always grew rucked and pebbled. The middle of the shinny rink was still sunken and would take another thousand litres from the hose. But both rinks would be ready by morning.

At first tonight the man hadn't been there. Then, maybe a half-hour ago, he'd appeared. She had to guess the time because she hadn't heard or seen him arrive. If this were one of her horror novels, he would be a ghost risen out of the earth of the old graveyard. She'd been easing the hose head back and forth, adrift in her night thoughts, which moved erratically, curving, burrowing, doubling back, unlike day thoughts, which had more practical places to get to, when she looked up and there he was, confronting the obelisk, closer to it tonight. . . . On the second night they'd exchanged hellos, nothing more. She'd sensed his deepening seriousness and concentration. Maybe he was getting frustrated, too. Or scared of failure. Did crazy men fear failure the way sane men did? Thinking of Gavin now.

All his short-lived ventures. His departure had been a relief in some ways—making a driven man feel important was an unfinishable job—but she missed him, too. Nights she did. For some moments she dwelled on missing Gavin in the nights. Then she looked up: hoarse, drunken shouting. Three kids, it looked like, crossing Balaclava Street, coming up the path. She was glad the man wasn't right on the path tonight. She'd lived here long enough to know trouble at a glance. They had the Grim Reaper look—slumpy, faceless, in layers of dark, baggy hooded sweatshirts. One of them had a biker jacket over his sweatshirt. Sure enough they came to a slouching halt on the path not far behind the man, who was facing away from them, apparently unaware. One of them, tall and skinny, was holding something like a crowbar. She shuffled out from behind the boards and stood in the open between the rinks, letting the water spray onto the patch of ice connecting them, keeping an eye on developments.

The taunts began—too slurred and soft, at first, to make out. The man didn't move or glance back. Maybe he was too deep inside his meditation, or felt he was on the verge of success. The kid in the biker jacket was edging up. "Hey, man. I've been hearing about you." His voice was firmer, clearer than the others': "Hey, stare at this, man." He shoved the man in the back, not hard, and the man did turn slowly, pivoting from the waist up. After a moment his dark, visored face tilted like a puzzled dog's.

"Leave him alone," she called.

The hooded faces turned to her in cartoon unison. In other circumstances it would have been funny. The man swivelled back into his posture. The kid in the biker jacket started right toward her, hands in his jacket pockets. In her stomach a down-rush of fear. The others followed him with slack, messy movements—they would have trouble when they reached the ice. She turned to face them as they came on through the half-light between the lampposts. She gave the control ring on the hose a half turn to reduce the flow and let the stream pool outward on the ice in front of her. The hose head was a half-foot of steel tapered to a flanged hole an inch and a half in diameter.

"He a friend of yours?" the leader called to her as he approached.

Gavin had been a connoisseur of confrontations and often gave his views on the best way to manage them. *You don't get into a war of words*, he used to say, addressing her as if she cared—actually just reassuring himself. *You let your opponent work himself into a state and talk away his wind. You stay calm and quiet and hold his stare.*

"Guess you must be friends," the leader called. "Neither of yous talk."

"What's that?" the tall one said.

"They're friends," the leader said. "The statue and the human Zamboni."

The sidekicks laughed, a crude, sloppy sound. They entered the perimeter of lamplight by the rinks and they were not kids. At a distance the baggy hooded shirts had made them look slighter, younger. They were in their twenties. It wasn't a crowbar the tall one held, it was the wooden handle of a mallet or sledge. Still advancing, the leader brought his hands out of his pockets and drew back his hood, slowly, with a sort of wry formality. He was smiling, lips closed. For a moment his face took up all her view. He was shockingly handsome. A twitch of attraction plunged downward with another spasm of fear, down into her womb, twin shocks, fused and unanimous in effect. It was a cruel face, beautiful. Strong brows, high-planed cheekbones, hooded grey eyes, plump lips inside a ring of stubble. The dark hair was brush cut, the skull knobbed as if muscled. She kept waving the hose slowly in front of her. The three stopped at the edge of the wet ice, just short of where the stream of water swept back and forth. Beads of spray sequined their trainers and lower pant legs.

"You were talking to us?" The voice was deep but nasal, grating, unsuited to that face.

"I just said leave him alone."

"It's you we want to see anyway." He looked up at her. After a moment his smooth brow crimped slightly, his eyes welled wider. He'd figured it out. He said nothing. It was the third one who said, "Is this, like, a *woman?*" He was short and concave, with a pocked face, and he seemed the drunkest or most stoned of the three.

"I don't know," the leader said. "Ask her yourself. Is there a lady in there?"

"Never fucking seen a *woman* doing a rink."

"I seen her," the tall one said. "Told me to get the fuck off the ice, last year."

"I was hardly here last year," she said.

"In that other park. Down Barrie."

"Well, I guess the ice wasn't ready," she said. She took a hopeful glance at the crazy man. He wasn't seeing any of this. She should retreat to the hut, call the police. Something stopped her. She was slow on her feet—hadn't run a step in years. At least out here there was the hose and the wet ice between her and them.

"Looks ready now," the third one said.

"What, *her?*" the tall one said with a stupid leer.

"The ice."

"Check it and see, Zach," said the leader. Zach, the short one, tried sliding onto the surface beyond the pooling water. His lead foot drove through crusted slush. He started to topple forward, waved his arms, slammed backward onto his elbows and ass. You could hear his bones on impact. He rolled over onto all fours—hands and knees—and stayed like that, head drooped.

"Okay, you can get up now," she said. "You're wrecking my work. You should be moving on."

"We'd like to see your office first," the leader said, ignoring his hurt friend.

"You're not going to."

"We already dropped in at the hut in that other park. Up in the Heights."

"Sure," she said.

"You think I'm lying?"

His face was pale. He seemed ready to pull out a scalp as proof. Walt Unger, a small, shyly talkative chain-smoker, would be flooding the rink in Rideau Heights.

Zach was back on his feet, rubbing his wet elbows with the opposite hands—a hurt little boy gesture. His wince was angry, yet he glanced timidly at the ice as if it were alive and likely to buck him off his feet if he moved. "*Bitch*," he said, but it didn't seem directed at her. That was good—she didn't have to respond.

"Let's go," the leader said, and for a soaring moment she believed that he was addressing his friends, telling them they were moving on. Then she felt his cold eyes pushing deeper into her.

"Lead the way," he said.

"If I go into that office, it'll be to call the cops. And there's nothing there. You think any of us bring money out here for a graveyard shift?"

He seemed to be giving this some thought. Then he said, "Your friend at the other rink did."

"What?"

"Brought money."

"I doubt that very much."

He went even whiter. "You know what?" he said, frowning, as if he had just discovered something that surprised him very much. "You're a goof."

"What?"

"A *goof.*"

Zach let a single laugh ride the silence. *Goof.* Not the A-word, not the B-word, not the C-word. Gavin had never done time like others in his family—he'd run a series of video and corner stores, trying and failing to franchise them—but a few of his boyhood friends had done time, and so he, of course, had considered himself an expert on Inside. And goof, he'd told her, was the worst thing you could call another inmate. Fucker, loser, asshole, shithead—that whole repertoire could get you into big trouble, no question, but goof was the worst. Maybe because it felt so silly. So *dismissive.* A fucker, after all, might fuck you, or fuck you up, or fuck you over. A goof was just pathetic. Maybe handsome here had done time. Certainly he'd done time. He knew how to use the word. But the use of the word bothered, *enraged* her, for another reason altogether and now she jerked the control ring fully open and turned the hose on him, narrowing the mouth with her gloved thumb so it sprayed even harder. *Bitch* she would have preferred. A bitch at least was female. Fat bitch, even. Bull dyke. Anything in that line. This was worse than being invisible, worse than being looked through or past, which happened all the time, and so be it, she could take it, a small daily heartbreak—things could be far worse. She doused him from the knees up, briefly but thoroughly, finishing at the face—how she resented that sculpted, cocky face!—then aimed the hose over at the tall one, but he and Zach were quickly shuffling backward off the ice.

The leader was rigid with the soaking—face twisted, shoulders hunched up, arms dangling. For a few moments his body stayed like that while his face slowly relaxed, refocused. He unzipped his jacket, reached in, pulled out a pair of red-handled ice picks, the sort snowmobilers use to pull themselves clear if they fall through the ice. One in each bare hand he came at her, his trainers stuttering over the wet ice. She turned the hose on him again. He kept coming, head lowered, squinting hard. The other two converged on her from either side with the same clumsy shuffle. She took her thumb off the outlet. The leader's face was shiny, sopping, his narrowed eyes fixed not on her eyes but lower—maybe her mouth or throat. His eyes had glazed over, unreachable. He was quivering. There was no use trying to talk. She was backing into the darker area between the lamppost and the warming hut, her heart punching at her ribs. She gripped the spouting hose head like a club. He lunged, swiping the picks in front of her face, then slipped forward, off balance. She didn't know whether to club or stab at him with the hose head but her body decided, thrusting at his face as it came up—the eyes wide—her full weight and strength behind it. Gavin's advice again. Never be tentative with a first blow. Though it hadn't helped Gavin in the end. He'd died three years back—four years after leaving her—in a confrontation on John Street, screaming in through the window of somebody's cube van until he dropped, his heart finally imploding with the decades of rage. He'd needed her after all, she realized. He relied on her outlook. To Ellen, anger was a rare detour, not a lifetime of highways.

She connected, but it was an odd feeling, blunted. Her attacker's face jerked down. The hose seemed stuck. In a panic she yanked back and he was sagging to his knees, dropping the ice picks, reaching for his face. The other two men stopped and froze.

"Shane?" the tall one said, voice shrivelling. "What'd she do to you, man?"

He was making coarse, braying sounds. She crouched down, holding the once-more streaming hose, grabbed the ice picks, put them in her outside pocket, stood up.

"Shane?" said Zach.

"My eye," he said. The words were muffled. He lowered his hands and turned his face up toward hers, his friends still behind him. She flinched and gasped— a ladylike sound—a lady in a film, about to faint.

She dropped the hose and knelt down. "Oh my God."

"Get away," he said.

"You," she said to the tall one, who was closest to the hut, "go in, call 9-1-1."

"9-1-1? Are you fucking joking, lady?"

Now she was a lady.

"We need an ambulance," she said.

"No way, they'll take us in."

"Just ask for an ambulance!"

"He'll be okay. Come on, Shane."

"My eye!"

Zach started toward her and Shane.

"Don't move!" she told him. "You might step on it."

"You mean . . . ?" His mouth was ajar, brows stitched together.

"We have to look for it. Call 9-1-1," she told the tall one. "Step carefully!"

He glanced over at Zach. Zach said, "We could like, call, then run for it."

"I need you both to help me look."

"They always send a cop car too," the tall one said.

"They can put it back in," she said, "the eye." She was pretty sure about this. She looked at the hut. She needed to turn off the water. It kept spewing from the hose lying at her knees, so water was lapping out around them, maybe carrying the eye further into the dark. But it couldn't have gotten far. Shane was on his side on the wet ice, curled up, rocking and grunting, one hand over the socket with its dangling nerve as she searched around him, tearing off her four gloves, peering hard, easing her hand over the ice. There were only a few spots of blood. No eye.

"Please," he whispered, "help me. I'm sorry."

"We'll find it," she said. "Tell your friend to call an ambulance! The tall guy."

"I need help, Gabe, call!"

Zach was shuffling around, hunched almost double, searching. "Pretty hard to see over this way," he said with the casual tone of a drunk looking for a dropped coin. Gabe picked his way toward the office door. Ellen was crawling over the puddled ice, tracing a circle around Shane. She would spiral outward in widening laps until she found the eye. She glanced over at the crazy man—still confronting the obelisk, oblivious. The door of the office swung open and light spilled onto the ice.

"That's good!" she called. "Leave it open."

"Hey, I think it's . . . shit. No." Zach was bent over, groping at something on the ice. As she watched, he toppled slowly forward.

Gabe was emerging from the office. In the doorway he stood silhouetted, panting as if he'd just run back from a distant payphone. Her new radio/CD player was in his hand. He shrugged, sheepish.

"I did call," he said. "I've got to go. Sorry, man."

She wasn't sure who he meant by that. Pushing with one foot, sliding with the other like a curler, he skittered away to where the ice ended at the path leading onto Bay Street. As he hit the pavement he began sprinting, impressively fast for an intoxicated man with a large object in one hand.

Zach, now on his hands and knees like her, had stopped looking for the eye. He was watching Gabe disappear. She figured he would take off now too—but then he went on searching.

She said, "Zach?"

"I'm Sh-shane." A whisper through jittering teeth.

The black leather of his jacket was frosting over.

"No, I mean your friend."

"Me?" said Zach. His head turned vaguely.

"Come more over this way—I doubt it could have got over to the boards."

"Be careful," Shane breathed, "they can put them back in."

She was moving away from Shane, outward in her circles. Then she thought she saw it. It had slid off a good twenty feet, to where the wet ice met the hard bank of snow shovelled to clear room for the rinks. It was in the shadow of that bank. She was sure now. She crawled toward it, trembling. The eye seemed to watch her with unnatural alertness, even a kind of indignation, as if she were too slow in coming to its aid. Closer still, it seemed to stare not at but through her, at something behind or beyond her.

"I think I see it!" Zach yelled. He must be watching where she was headed.

"Go into the hut," she called back. "There are bags in there, plastic bags in a Kleenex box, by your feet on the right as you go in. Get one and fill it with snow and bring it here. No, just bring it here. There's snow here."

"Okay! Just a minute!"

"You found it," Shane said behind her.

"You'll be all right," she said. She reached for the eye, then paused, wanting to put her rubber glove on. The glove was back on the ice beside Shane. She didn't touch the eye. She might damage it. It was hideous but riveting. Disembodied eyes made occasional appearances in horror novels, but those eyes were usually conscious, vigilant, a threat. This one was glassing over, as if losing interest in the world. Maybe starting to freeze. It didn't look real. Porcelain with an iris of grey-blue glass, and too perfectly round to be real. If this were a film she would complain about the special effects. Like when the Twin Towers fell, soon after Gavin's death—how it looked less real than the artificial disasters in films.

She wasn't sure how soft an eye was—her impression was that the main material was more or less like pudding, though held firm by a membrane. She could imagine her fingerprint remaining on the eye, a pattern he would look through for the rest of his life. She would wait for the bag of snow and ease it in with a knuckle.

A far howl of sirens, the sound slowly mounting. She stayed on her knees, huddled low over the eye as if to shield it from the cold. She cupped it with her shivering hands without making contact. This way she didn't have to see it. She glanced back. Zach had paused as he reached Shane on his way to the hut. He stood wobbling above his friend.

"You're going to pull through, dude."

"The hut!" she cried. "I need that bag!"

"Okay." He staggered on, almost fell again. Then his head tilted with a drunk's abrupt, temporary alertness. He'd heard the sirens. They were closing in. He ducked into the hut and emerged briskly, as though instantly sober, and slid toward her across the ice. The whites of his eyes showed larger. She had her left hand out for the bag and he relayed it to her with his stretched right.

For a second he stood above her, captivated by the eye. He glanced back at Shane. "I got to get out of here," he whispered loudly, then stepped up on the bank and tore away across the park—the opposite direction from Gabe—his shoulders pitching and his hood peeling back. He ran past the obelisk, the man there turning his head stiffly to watch him go. As the moaning of the sirens merged into a single scream, she stuffed a handful of snow into the bag—they were kept in the hut for picking up the dog turds that cluttered the park and sometimes the ice. With the knuckle of her index finger she nudged the eye over the lip of the bag. It rolled right in. Unsure whether to seal the bag or leave it open, she turned and crawled back toward Shane. She was afraid of standing—she might slip, drop the bag, even fall on it. She crawled on her knees and right hand, her left holding the bag clear.

Shane sat up as she approached. The back of the hand covering the empty socket was blue and unbloodied. His good eye was fixed on hers. He was seeing her now, really looking. One of those rare times. Sometimes life seemed little else than a struggle to win the attention, the gaze, of others. That was what Gavin had really been doing, she supposed, screaming into that van at the end.

The ambulance and two squad cars flashed into sight, driving east on Ordnance. They would circle around and enter the park from Bay Street, by the hut. They vanished again but their sirens went on ripping the air apart.

"It's going to be all right, I think," she said, reaching him.

"If I can just keep my eye."

"You will."

"I'm sorry."

"They'll have that face of yours up and running in no time."

She wasn't sure if this was true. She'd almost said *good-looking face*.

"If I have to go back inside," he said, slurring the words through purple lips, "I can take it, but not blind. Can I see it?"

"Guess you'd better confirm we've got the right one," she said.

His torso jerked, as if shaken by a single laugh. She opened the bag. "Oh . . . Jesus," he said, stared back at by himself. She set her bare hand on his shoulder. His body trembled under the leather. The folds in the lap of his low-crotched jeans were frozen so it looked like he had an erection. He didn't flinch or look at her—he wouldn't now.

"Did you hurt Walt, at the other rink?"

"Not like this. Hardly at all."

"That better be true." She gripped his hood and pulled it roughly onto his head.

"And for t-t-twenty bucks. Nobody could believe my life."

With a face like that? she heard herself think. The crass assumption she now sometimes shared, that life must be a June breeze for the nice-looking. As if her life had been easy in her teen years. Shane would have been all over her then, and she would have craved him for the danger in his look. Why had nature given bad men all the attractive vitality? Like Gavin, years ago. Why did horror and romance so often overlap? She pushed her hand further, around his shoulder, feeling uncomfortably huge next to him. He seemed about to rest his head against her arm, then pulled back. A wall of hard, hot light came at them as the ambulance and squad cars shrieked up behind. To shield her eyes, she ducked her face, got a closer look at him. He seemed to be going into shock. His good eye stared off to where their twinned shadow was fast lengthening over the ice and the shrouded park. The crazy man was lit up at the edge of the headlights' fanning swath. Turned toward them at last, he seemed to be staring, his posture solemn, noncommittal, his baseball cap in his hands like a mourner. "You're going to be all right," she told Shane, though really she wanted to take him by the chin and roughly turn his face toward hers and say, "Look at me."

[NOUGHTS & CROSSES]

an unsent reply

-------Original Message-----
From: <j.in.corydon@hotmail.com>
To: <nella_biagini@sympatico.ca>
Sent: April 22, 2007 1:16 AM
Subject: RE: Hello?

n,

yes yes i did get your email but needed to reflect a little. i'm
sorry. and yes i do think it might be best if i pulled back a
little now. i seem to need some space to hear my own
breathing, my own thoughts. it is hard when we are always in
dialogue. i am sorry if this feels abrupt or my reasons feel
vague, they just must be. for one thing, as i guess i implied, i
have been asked to keep secrets and want to keep my word.
i know you understand. you, after all, are one of my secrets.

and as you know yourself and even said, maybe a severing, a temporary severing is what's best now, for both of you. for everyone involved. please don't worry about me, i will be all right, i am determined to get through this time. i promise i will get in touch again when i feel i can.

love always,

j

—

n

As in: never again, never again. That phrase with its cardiac cadence. Slight arrhythmia. A certain tunnelled clump of muscle misbehaving, missing steps or taking clumsy extras, a drunk at the top of the stairs in the dark. When you used the abbreviation before, that n, it was an intimate act, an adoring diminutive, as though to make the beloved compact enough to carry with you secretly. You always found me tall for a woman (too tall?). Now it's as though you want to avoid repeating my full name: Arnella. Nelli. nell. n. To deduct the name down to nothing. Nobody, no one, nowhere, nothing, nought, null, nil.

yes yes

The one thing you would never say in the act was *Yes!* It was always *O no O no O no O no!* when you were getting close, and when I asked if it was because something was wrong, this "thing" was wrong, or was your pleasure

(I would like to think so) intense to the point of pain, you turned shy and said it was "just what came out—you know" (your favourite lazy phrase) "like when a song shows up in your head and you just, like, let it out?" I didn't press the point. I sensed you retreating into your separate memoir of intimate events. I didn't ask if that was what *always* "came out," or only with me. Separate memoirs, former loves. How crowded our bedrooms are these days. (Or not. Not my bedroom. Not these days.) For over a century there was a tunnel extending from the crypt of the main cathedral here down to the Hôtel Dieu, the old Catholic hospital, so the nuns and priests could stay indoors in winter when they were called off to see sick parishioners or perform the last rites. A few weeks ago I read about it and for some reason kept wanting to tell you. Why not now? Forty years ago they decided the tunnel was becoming unsafe. They sealed it off at both ends, but the passageway is still there, thirty feet under Brock Street, totally dark, of course, and empty. Sometimes now when I'm alone it hits me.

reflect a little

Five days of this little reflecting. Here is what gnaws me, besides the after-effects of five days of little reflecting on your part and much waiting on mine. What gnaws and haunts me is: whatever passed through your mind in those five (plus) days, all the stuff you decided not to voice, reconsidered, revised, rejected then retrieved, reneged on again, at last deleted. I want it back, the full census of your reflections, a crammed CT-scanful, all those references to me, I can't accept that they're gone, neural flickers like email never sent or lost in transit somewhere in the digital ether we're all adrift in now. Or: whispers of a couple passing in that tunnel before it was sealed. A pair of nuns, let's say, lovers on the down low, erotically revved up by the proximity of illness, death. Death's weirdly elating ultimacy. Did they have torches? A medieval image, cinematic to the point of camp: dark figures hunched, capes wafting, torches in hand, flapping down limestone corridors propped with timber stays for safety, as in a mine shaft. Our lovers must feel unnerved, even so. They are crossing so many lines. The anxiety of the crime makes one notice other dangers everywhere. And safety measures always seem to whisper: *some day we will fail!* It feels safer where there are no measures. And either way, in their presence or absence, no safety.

i'm sorry
Sorry, maybe, because there *were* no reflections? You'd made up your mind? You're sorry that you stalled about breaking the news, is all? They say that from the bottom of a deep hole you can see the stars shining even at noon. I never trust those little factlets from the *Globe;* still, it's good news for the dead.

and yes i *do* think it might be best
Italics mine. But even without the italics (it's my ethnic

privilege to overuse them) your implication here is that *I made the suggestion in the first place!* Actually, of course, I did: "If you need me to pull back now, I will." Naturally I didn't mean it, though. Didn't want you to *accept*. Wanted you to say *O no O no O no O no!* What's more, *you must have known I didn't mean it*—you just pretended to take the words at face value to give yourself a convenient out. Lovers are the world's only honest people, according to certain poets and sages. Ho ho ho. I'm nostalgic for the salad days, grad and postgrad in the late '70s and early '80s, York and UBC, when it was an article of faith (if not experience) in our circle that straight lovers, bourgeois lovers, were the only dishonest ones. *T[he] on/lie dys/honest ones.*

That stage of life when confidence depends on culprits.

Oh, to have both back.

i seem to need some space

But, but I thought we were bitter opponents of platitudes, you and I; we agreed that our love was *not like any other love* (italics mine, quotation yours, email 64, line 17: I am now chief archivist of your intimacies), and to consecrate and, as you would say, "honour" this singularity, we agreed that we would never speak of our love in clichés. We smogged the air with exalted vows like that. Teenage summer lovers in a song by the Boss. So, maybe a return to cliché is a neatly symmetrical way to shut things down . . . to *deconsecrate* our love, the way they do with those churches whose flocks have died off or moved to Palm Beach, and the buildings are converted to meeting halls or museums or daycares. Ever wondered how they deconsecrate a cathedral? I really should know, after a quarter-century in my field. (A century, one learns, is a small thing.) A choir assembles for the last time, chanting in discord, an infernal chorus. At the altar a bishop exhausts the full roster of religious obscenities. The organist, wild-eyed, riffs on anthem-rock standards, Queen, Gary Glitter, The Sweet, as if playing at a hockey rink.

j, my j, you've *recanted.*

Shouldn't "recant" mean to sing again?

to hear my own breathing

If I woke in the night, the precious nights I had you here, I was always taken aback at how hard it was to detect your breaths. Even when you were deeply out (pretty much always) your breathing was delicate; once or twice I almost panicked, you know how the mind works at night, and there were always those footlights of unease around our meetings, fear of your husband interrupting our, uh, tutorial with a call, so that panic would feed on puny fears and several times I actually put the back of my hand to your open mouth to feel the breaths. Then my mouth next to yours to breathe them in. That close, I found you breathing, of course, calm and profound, with a faint sighing wheeze in your lungs, under your bare breasts, which were pillowed one over the other as you lay furled on your side. Your breath smelled fine, spicy, with a subtle finish of garlic and Syrah. Then one night it changed. That's how I knew we were coming to an end. More conventional signs had materialized as well—your canned laughter, diluted gaze, undilated pupils—but *that* was how I knew: the last two nights your breath turned unfamiliar in your sleep. Changes deep inside, where I couldn't reach. I wonder about the air in that blocked tunnel, after forty years of disuse. Is oxygen stable or does it deteriorate over time? I wouldn't know. Your husband would. Could toxic fumes have seeped in through the limestone? If the ends were unblocked tonight, could we still walk through it and breathe? How long does a closed-off tunnel remain a possible route?

always in dialogue

To you it may have felt that way. You're the one with other allegiances. (More of them, maybe, than I thought.) A day came when I abandoned my latest stalled article to check email—still dial-up then—maybe thirty times, hoping for a reply. You must have been reflecting a little. Finally I just remained online, waiting. I answered a few other "urgent" emails that I'd left to ripen for days, maybe weeks. That took some time. I've never learned, like you, to crash out a reply, in lowercase, in the current electronic shorthand that I am still not used to—insulting!—though I see it all the time from my students :) Did those. Waited. Stared at the empty inbox and willed a message to appear. For quite some time I stuck it out. Funny, I've never once sat staring at the phone, though you would sometimes call me. Staring at a phone seems somehow goofier. A screen is meant to be stared at. Things are meant to appear there. Maybe I could *induce* you to write me. Eventually I took the modem cord and slunk the three flights down to the lobby and locked it in the morgue-like drawer of my mailbox. Came upstairs for a double Campari and soda. Left the cord down there for a good half-hour.

i am sorry if this feels abrupt or my reasons feel vague, they just must be
Oh and another nice thing about email: you are always sitting down to read it. No more Puccini swoons, buckling to the floor with the farewell letter clinched in one hand, the other cupping the brow. Instead, you settle deeper in your chair. The world stops entering your mind through the senses. You've been sealed off with your obsession, and shame. *my reasons . . . must be kept vague.* I always knew there were truths you wouldn't tell me, so I avoided entering certain corridors of inquiry; but there was also an implication, about the two of us, that we just *knew*—we UNDERSTOOD. William Burroughs said that gay love differs from straight love because a queer lover ("homosexual" was how he put it, I believe) always knows what the other is thinking and feeling, while a straight lover

never does. Hmmm . . . better that I did my thesis on Bloomsbury and Woolf, instead of (a quip over cocktails, long ago) "Bloomsbury & the Beats: Points of Unexpected Comparison."

as i guess i implied

Didn't we make a pact never to *do* this sort of thing? To *guess* and *imply?* To become, in each other's sight, hazy at the margins by delivering half-truths? That's how people deconsecrate themselves, from human into something less. Spectres. Cyborgs. Didn't I mention this opinion? Not that you listened well, ever. Speaking of blockages. Consider the ears of the egotist . . . Now, as I listen, trying to peer through this blockage, I wonder if you are alone. There's your husband, of course, but he doesn't count. Two daughters. Neither do they. For the purpose of this madness only *somebody else* counts. (Especially if female.) You told me I was the first woman you had been with. Is there another now? Have I created a monster?

i have been asked to keep secrets

The cathedral's literature (I went and took one of their free tourist leaflets; lit a lampion for the hell of it) gives no clue as to how, or with what, the passageway was sealed.

i know you understand

See above under Burroughs, William.

you, after all, are one of my secrets
One of your . . . excuse me? I thought this was an exclusive engagement! Now I'm no longer your secret, I'm *one* of your secrets? Um, are your secrets a *clique* now? A *category?* A *women's collective?* All on the same level . . . Maybe your secrets should be more civil about this. Maybe they should all get *used* to one another. Your secrets are "all in this together". . . no rank, no priority, no hierarchy of closeness . . . it's a sorority, a full *democracy* of secrets! The one exact thing that love isn't.

as you know yourself
Oh, I do. One of us had to end it. The question is: who began it, Janet? Another reference that dates me and, by omission, you. We have all the particulars. The year (2002). The season (summer). The place (Kingston). The course (Religious Imagery in Popular Culture and Contemporary Women's Fiction), and you in semi-attendance to steal time—admit it, finally, you're a dabbler, a summer slummer—away from your aphasic husband and colicky twins. When you went back to Winnipeg in the fall, I assumed it was over, but the thing wouldn't die. Since then I've propped everything on your annual holiday here in the Thousand Islands.

maybe a severing
New word for an old context. Feels more honest than "spend a little time apart," anyway. And honesty is what

we all want at such times. But *severing*—there is a hard word. I'd never noticed the "severe" in it before. Or really heard the sound of it before. *SEVering*. The oiled blade sliding down to separate head from body with a blunt, chunky sound.

a temporary severing

Whew! For a minute there I thought it was permanent! As if it was in the very *nature* of severings to be that way . . . But a moment's reflection allows us to generate any number of counter-examples. In the fatal crash, the victim's spinal cord was *temporarily* severed. As the glaciers retreated, rising sea waters *temporarily* severed Asia from North America. Alas, it proved necessary to sever the miner's gangrenous limb *temporarily*. Somehow the bungee jumper's cord was severed in mid-leap—*but only temporarily!*

for both of you

You always wrote your emails fast, furtively, late at night or early in the morning, and there were always misspellings or little misnomers like this one. "Both of *us*," I assume you meant. You and me. Because there aren't two people hereabouts, in my world, my room. All the same . . . maybe you did half-mean that *I've* been as split apart as you. Between wanting to respect your family commitments and wanting you all to my lonesome? Nope: between wanting *not* to violate the current student–teacher protocol (which I always supported and still believe in and which the dying white males of the department, just them, allegedly, still flout when they can) and wanting to violate, repeatedly, you.

for everyone involved
Everyone! How did they get into this again? How I detest them! From the moment a love starts, Everyone is clamouring to get in, huffing and prodding, mobbing the door that a new couple seals fast and barricades—Everyone trying to peep through, push through, leaving messages, making demands. I should have known Everyone would get to us. They always do. Over and over I've lived my life for those days before they do.

i am determined to get through this time
The ambiguity! It makes me insane! How many times have I been over this one, trying to uncrate it? You are determined to ride out this painful, severe time in your life? Or: you are determined, *this* time, to get through? Let it be the first option! Let it be that this hurts you as much as it hurts me. Let this not be yet another unacceptable revelation—that our affair wasn't your first of the kind. You said it was. Now you might be saying that there was another time and you *didn't* get through it—never got over her. (Or him.) Other times? Who? Who? This vision of multitudes barging into your inbox, your bedroom, your body.

i will get in touch again when i feel i can
What's this if not a melodramatic way of saying, Don't
call us, we'll call you? My people will call your people.
My multitudes will call your solitude . . . but don't hold
your breath. (Whatever remains in that sealed place.)
Cave exploration is something you always said you
wanted to try out. I can hardly bear to use the correct,
ridiculous term. Spelunking. I spelunk, you spelunk.
We will spelunk. She had spelunked. So we'll go no
more spelunking. Partly this is why I keep bringing up
that sealed tunnel—not as some elaborate genital met-
aphor, but because I know you would be interested and
maybe want to explore it. Count me out, though.
Daredevils come in aerial or subterranean form. How
many folks do you know who have both skydived and
spelunked? Doesn't happen. When you would talk
about spelunking, I would counter with skydiving, my
own potential death-wish hobby. We had to compro-
mise on the earth's surface—on driving *really, really fast*
those few times when we were far from Everyone
together. Rental cars are good for that: convertibles.
A *Thelma & Louise* outtake, except people probably
took me for your aunt, or duenna. Remember the
highway into the Cypress Hills? How amazed you were
that such committed flatness could collect itself into
hills—small mountains, our ears popping as we drove—
the way your life seemed to be climbing up from the
plains of your comfortable present onto high ridges of
possibility . . .

love always
But there's hope here, isn't there, there's not just a name, and not just "love"—no, it's "love always," even if there *is* the one conspicuous, crushing change, the absence of your usual starburst of xxxxxooooo. Or xoxoxoxo. It always varied. I go back through the emails now (printed out, of course—there's a paper trail after all, sweetie, though you prudently avoided writing letters)— I pore over them again, studying, tabulating the details of the x and o firework finale of all your emails, one hundred and fifty-eight in all, but especially the last twenty or so. I am trying to track the decline. How does the end enter? Where does it get in? In your most passionate note (I won't say email), right after the Cypress Hills Escapade, there were no less than ten x's and seven o's. (Why fewer o's than x's? Why *stint* like that on the o's? And what *are* x's and o's anyway? Kisses and embraces, embraces and kisses. We argued about which were which. To both of us it seemed obvious, a matter of common sense and common knowledge, and we were stunned, in a loving way, by the other's ignorance. You said, "O is the lips open for a deep kiss, X is the arms crossed over the embraced lover's back." Touched by this effort I replied, "Ingenious but wrong. O is the circle of the embracing lover's arms, X is the eye of the lover, the eyes, closed, X-ed out in the rapture of the kiss.") Love as a game of noughts and crosses. Nine emails before the end, I find *all my love, j, xxxooooxx*. Again this marked privileging of x over o. (Five and

three.) Five messages before the end, *Love forever, j, xxxxoo.* (Four and two.) Three messages before the end, o makes something of a comeback, outnumbering x for the first time in many missives, *Love, j, ooxxxooo.* In fact, the total number of signs here, eight, suggests if anything a strengthening of passion! Next, email 156, where o makes its final strong showing, *my love, j, ooxoo*—with the lone x almost lost among those still fervent hugs (or kisses???). Number 157, the second-last, shows this tic-tac-toe showdown entering its end-game, though the salutation—*yours always, j, ox*—almost seems to cancel out that lack.

j

I'm to be spared the final humiliation. You'll remain j to me, not Janet-Marie. In signing off, you could have withdrawn that intimate, tiny link between us, that hook lodged in my heart, and keyed in your full name. You chose not to; something does remain unsevered. And after all, if the Greek in the labyrinth (you never remember the names), slowly unreeling his ball of yarn so he could find his way back, had accidentally cut the thread—maybe on a cornering wall, a knife-edge of stone—he might have sensed it break and then groped his way back in the darkness, feeling for the lost end, splicing the yarn, persevering. We're back in the tunnel, you see. Despite my fear, I think I would go down and explore it with you, if they ever opened it up again. I am drawn to a fantasy of fucking you there, maybe in a side tunnel or cul-de-sac, tugging you away from the tedious tour group with its silly costumed guide to make slow, wordless love in the kind of darkness that people never really do it in. What would that be like? To have not the faintest glimpse or inkling of the one beside you, above you, below you? So the orgasm I'd give you, the way you liked it best, would star the gloom, seeming to project on the walls a brief, grand, enveloping galaxy. There we would be our own source of light. I don't want to see anything now. Darkness is far from the worst. Your note is very short. Worst is the whiteness of most of the printout under that j. So I've filled it and other pages, your faithful annotator and emptied teacher, with these notes, endnotes, that our dialogue not die.

[FIREMAN'S CARRY]

In memory of John Chappelle, 1954–2007

We shoulder the coffin of my friend Warren Reed down the front steps of the church and on toward the hearse's gaping back door. It reminds me of the receiving mouth of a crematorium, that door—how a coffin will glide through and into the discreetly quiet, white-hot furnace beyond. I always wonder how they manage to keep such a ravenous blaze so quiet.

I've read somewhere that fire, to certain ancient peoples, was an animal, as alive and on the same level as humans, horses, birds, fish, insects, everything. It's easy—especially for someone who has fought fires, and walked inside them—to imagine how the belief arose. Fire breathes air, like us. Fire eats wood as well as the flesh of animals, the dead as well as the living. It moves on its own, it has a voice and a vocabulary, it can seed itself and propagate, it can hibernate deep in the roots of trees and fully revive, it leaves a sort of bodily waste behind, it attacks, it withdraws, it can be tamed and domesticated, and finally, when it has eaten everything, it starves or else smothers or perishes by drowning. I've read, too, about a certain desert tribe who believed that while animals understood the language of fire, humans had somehow lost it, along with the other animal tongues—but that each person at the moment of death regained the capacity to understand. This tribe believed their dead should never be buried but instead burned, so the living flames could guide and sing the dead into the afterlife.

There will be no flames today, though—no furnace door. Firefighters seldom incline to the crematory option. Once we load my friend into the hearse, we'll be getting into our cars and merging into the motor-cade heading out to the cemetery on the outskirts of town, or what used to be the outskirts. Green and peaceful, breezy grounds, tall, stately hardwoods two centuries old.

My friend's maple coffin is—do I need to say this?— heavy on our shoulders, though it's not the burden it might be for an average pallbearer. There are six of us, and the five who wear full dress uniform (I'm the odd one out, in my formal civvies) are all in good shape, the way I used to be when I was signing in to the fire hall gym four times a week and carrying serious poundage into and out of burning buildings.

Then there's the fact that we're getting *used* to bearing these coffins and sliding them into hearses. It's not what you might think, either—not fatalities on the job, floors and burning walls collapsing, chemical explosions. An occupational epidemic of cancer is what it is, cancer of the brain, cancer of the liver, plenty of lung cancer, pancreatic cancer, cancer from all the burning crud we're inhaling in all the factories, garages, condos and offices we try to save. Still, my friend feels heavy in his coffin, this virtually bombproof carapace whose protection he could have used in life, on the job, but now has zero use for.

I left the department over a year ago. I'm doing sedentary work now, not exciting, but it's a job, it's safe, it pays decently, and to tell the truth I rarely miss the challenge and adrenal rush of what I used to love doing. Plus I work at home, meaning more family time and none of the strife and stress of working with others. That endless chafing of personalities. It was an awkward resignation, if you can call it that. (Did I fall or was I pushed? A bit of both. If I'd wanted to fight it, the union could have saved my job, I'm pretty sure, maybe after moving me to another hall.)

So we ease my friend into the hearse and there's a curious interlude, nobody sure who should close the back door. Standing beside us in a too-big black suit, the funeral director's assistant—a thin, fidgety kid who looks like he should be slouching along in loose jeans and an undershirt—hesitates too. Is it his job to close the door? This might be his first funeral. For a moment we stand looking around, then downward, the crew at their own spit-buffed parade boots, me at my laceless, matte-black shoes, shoes shaped like a platypus's bill. They're clean and new, not too informal, I feel, though suddenly I wonder. A couple of my ex-crewmates are having a look at them, and they seem to baffle the giant crew captain, Jack Steiger. He and I never got along too well, especially at the end. And yet he surprised me yesterday by calling and gruffly inviting me to join the rest of the crew as a pallbearer. Most people, I've come to see, surprise you more often, not less, as they get older.

Big Steiger aims a look of hard inquiry at the apprentice and nods at the door. The kid, helpless in the face of such raw, animal ascendancy, steps forward and swings it closed.

Room 303 was the last one I broke into, during my last fire, my last night on the job. I'd clomped upstairs in the dark with Reed and Steiger, full gear, hose and lifeline, breathing loud and laboured inside the mask. From between the room's floorboards and out of the joins between the wainscoting and walls, spotlit by my headlamp, smoke hissed up in gauzy sheets that broke apart at waist level, scrolling and spreading through the room. And there was *purple* smoke, like a stage effect at a heavy metal show. A rooming house is about the worst place for a fire, short of a chemical factory. Narrow hallways, the wiring below code, a dozen rooms or more, each warehoused with the kind of fodder that fires dote on— aged mattresses, bales of newspapers and *Reader's Digest*, paperbacks, LPs, dry-rotted furniture. This place was sensationally decrepit. Shredded Insulbrick over century-old clapboard. Packed with flammables and going up in a whoosh. We had four trucks out front, ladders deployed, crews fighting to dent the firestorm that had already blown out the lower windows, seeking more oxygen, more space to expand. The crews were spraying from all angles, triangulating the fire's heart, trying to buy us a few minutes upstairs. In the south alley, another hose was drenching the side-door stairwell where we'd entered and where we hoped to exit, soon. For now the lower flight of stairs was a foaming, ter-raced cascade, like a salmon weir.

There were five of us inside. Truba and Santos were on the second floor and they would be moving fast, I knew, making sure the rooms were vacated and if pos-sible rescuing any pets. Reed, Steiger and I had climbed to the third floor on the same mission.

It's remarkable how many people take the time to lock their doors when fleeing a major fire. As if the whole event might be a burglar's ruse. And it happens more often, not less, in the poorer buildings. We didn't give the place any odds of surviving, and if it did survive it would be demolished, so I wasted no time putting my axe to the door, a necessity I always enjoyed: the arc and acceleration of the heavy blade overhead, powered by you and at the same time pulling your arms along for the ride, the big, gratifying crunch as you connect at the targeted spot, usually to the inside of the handle.

The door of 303 burst open, one blow. Though these old doors were solid, not veneer—crafted with conscience in a conscientious time—the wood around the lock was rotten, the whole structure weakened by a few dozen tenancies of constant opening, closing, slamming. I heard another door splinter nearby. As I pushed into the room, Reed, up the hall, was calling through his portable that there was a cat in 306. Steiger called back, "Grab it and let's move." I peered into 303. Those hissing plies of floorboard smoke were hypnotic. It still wasn't too smoky to see: a fridge and, surprisingly, a freezer too. Red sleeping bag on a mattress on the floor, square Arborite table with an ashtray and two beer cans, a plastic church-hall chair. A steel dolly, the kind used to move large appliances. The pasteboard wardrobe seemed to be full of fancy stuff: swaths of what looked like red velvet, black silk. And on the floor beside it, two extra-large black plastic bags, as if for industrial garbage. Bags of tires?

I'm not sure why I did it—Steiger was hollering again that we had to move—but I walked over and investigated. I parted the thick, unsecured lips of the first bag and jerked back in disgust: a dark, scaled coil as thick as my upper arm. No need to feel it. I knew it was alive, or had been until moments ago—nobody lives in a single room with enormous dead snakes, though sharing the place with living ones seems almost as crazy. I backed away, turned and came out the door just as Steiger reached it.

"Something in there? We got to move now." There was a problem with the voice amp of his mask. His voice was faint, tinny—a worked-up announcer broadcasting warnings on a distant radio.

"No, sir," I shouted. "Yes. Snakes. Two, I think. Big ones. Huge."

His eyes widened behind the mask. Reed loomed out of the smoke, a Siamese cradled in his arms, oddly silent, its squinted blue eyes running. Reed said, "What is it, Terr?"

"Snakes. Big ones. Maybe we should bring them?"

"They moving?" Steiger asked.

"No."

"Probably dead. Can't be worrying about snakes."

"Got to get this cat out," Reed said, and he lumbered toward the stairs.

"And dangerous," Steiger said. "Let's go."

"I don't think they're dead, sir."

"Now!" Steiger said, and I followed him.

We pounded down the sodden, steaming last flight to the door. Heat radiated through the inner wall, fire on the other side. We clicked out our regulators. Truba and Santos stood squared in front of the door, blocking it like riot police. A small man, facing them, wanted to get past. He hopped once, comically, surprisingly high, trying to see over them. He was bald on top and the greying fringe of his hair was a fright wig of long, tangled curls. A gaunt, excited face—yet the left side of it was passive. He was yammering in French but his urgency didn't budge the drooping half of his face, which looked years younger, lineless, uninvolved. Reed, with the weeping Siamese, pushed past this standoff and then Steiger did too. I shouldered in between Truba and Santos, adding my width to their wall. I grew up in Montreal and knew some French. Maybe I could help. The man wanted something from his room. This always happens, especially with the older, poorer victims. I said, "*Puis-je vous aider, monsieur?*" and he paused for a moment, startled, then thrust his contorted face at me and screamed, "*Sauvez mes serpents!*"

"Those are *your* snakes," I said in English. He was shouting in French again and I made out a few details. He performed in clubs, at fairs, circuses. He and his serpents. They were how he earned his bread. He was in town for only a few months. He should never have come here.

"*Ils sont dangereux, vos serpents?*"

"*Non, absolument pas!*" he cried, and again he tried pushing past us.

Truba was getting the gist of the French. "Fuck his snakes," he said. "Nobody's going back in for a fucking snake." And he leaned down over the man, his big gloved hand pointing upward as he enunciated, full volume, "Danger—okay?"

"I don't care about it!" the man said with a dense accent. "*Ils sont ma vie!*"

Steiger was back. The heat was scorching through my gear now, into my shoulders and spine. Truba and Santos and I, and now Steiger, were a human bulkhead protecting this lunatic from the killing heat. Down one side of his double face—half-frenzied, half-resigned—tears streamed, lit silver by our headlamps, which were all focused on him. I felt for him. Steiger didn't.

"Man wants his snakes," Santos announced.

"Get him out of here," Steiger roared. "Your snakes are all gone, okay? It's over! Christ, this is a four-alarm fire!"

Steiger is a giant, like I said, a buzz-cut linebacker of a man with a big, groomed Asterix the Gaul moustache that hides his mouth even when he's yelling commands. Once, in a competition, he bore two of the smaller men in a fireman's carry, one over each shoulder. The most daunting man I've ever met. Even the platoon chief shies up around him. Though I'm not a big guy myself, I've never been the type to scare—but let Steiger, with those cold-forged eyes, level one of his alpha glowers at you and something folds up in your soul. It's a myth that bullies lack self-esteem. Most bullies have plenty. I never took to Steiger, never liked his crude sarcasm about my choice of books and movies in the fire hall, and now I deeply disliked how he was giving the Look to this little man. I could see it: behind the man's eyes the resolve was wilting and I hated to

see it die, that rare, rallied courage, stronger than
adrenaline, that gives anyone heroic strength for a short
while. It might come never, or once in a lifetime, maybe
more often for a woman, giving birth (I was there both
times and saw it in Tricia, especially with our first-
born—a state beyond mere inspiration). Battling fires,
I guess I've gotten there more often than most, twice
helping to rescue the children of strangers, and one
time also when my younger girl was brushing a horse
in its stall and it shifted and pinned her, I leapt in and—
so I hear—grappled that thousand-pound mare away
from her and against the back wall.

Those states of pure, fearless purpose helped keep
me in the crew for a long time—kept me there even
with Steiger as captain. Though if it hadn't been him,
it might have been someone else. There's always someone around to set you straight. To let you in on God's
private view about where to draw the line between
what counts down here and what doesn't. As for the
official line: we save people or we die in the attempt.
Dogs or cats if we can do it without dying. Budgies
and gerbils if it's possible and convenient. Reptiles, I
guess, not at all.

So Steiger kept bawling at the man, who kept plead-
ing back in a flinching little voice, and the heat went
on building inside my suit. I fixed my gaze on the snake
man's face so as not to let Steiger catch and command
my eye. Then I turned and splashed back into the stairwell, clicking my regulator into place. The inner walls

were slick, sweating grease and creosote. Behind me, a moment of near quiet—then Steiger was ordering me to get my ass back outside and the snake man was yapping instructions in a hopeful, higher voice. Steiger thumping in behind me. I was taking the steps two at a time, no hose, no lifeline. At the first turning I saw Steiger peripherally, at the bottom of the stairwell, glaring up, hollering in a voice ragged with anger and disbelief. Someone was disobeying him.

The smoke was heavier now. I glanced up the second-floor hallway: smoke from under the doors that Truba and Santos had closed when they fled. The last flurry of words the snake man had pitched at me settled into sense: Don't worry. *Ils ont mangé.* They've eaten. They're sleeping. *Ils dorment dans leurs sacs.*

By floor three I was winded again. No one would last long up here without a mask, but the snakes still had a prayer, down on the floor, in a dormant state, *léthargiques, tu comprends?*, inside those bags. I pushed open the hacked door of 303 and ducked low, under the worst of the heat and smoke, and then got down on all fours. Sometimes in the final stages you have to wriggle on your stomach, a frogman searching the murky floor of a lake. My headlamp showed about two metres. I found the first bag and rose into a crouch and peeked in—that unmoving, monstrous coil—then gathered the neck of the bag in a chokehold. I was counting on heavy and it was. I remembered the dolly across the room but knew I might not find it in this smoke. I turned my back to the bag, braced my hands over my shoulder, heaved. I had the bag sealed but I hated not being able to see it. Understand this much—I wasn't acting out of sentimentality. I've never cared for snakes. I'm more the mammal type. Horses, cats, big goofy retrievers.

I rose with a grunt that I felt more than heard, then stumped to the door, keeping as low as possible. I wasn't sure if there was movement inside the bag or if it was just the contents slopping against my back. A hundred and twenty pounds, at least. I almost crashed into Steiger, who filled the doorway.

"We have to get out now!" The voice from his mask was minuscule, shaky. I couldn't make out the face under the headlamp. The little voice commanded, "*Leave* the goddamned snake! These floors could go any time!"

"I'm not leaving it, sir," I said. It helped that his face was hidden. It helped that my voice, a bellow inside my mask, now dwarfed his. "And I'll come back for the other if the floors hold." I trudged toward him, to get past. What else could I do? It's not like I was suddenly fearless. Not at all. There was the fire, there was Steiger, there was a huge tropical constrictor coiled a few inches from my throat. But where I draw the line now is nowhere. Alive is alive. Why let a thing die for being what it can never help but be?

Steiger moved aside. I made for the stairs, my eyes scalded with sweat. A low, immense, steady moaning welled up from beneath us, as if the building were giving up the ghost—the sound of a fire that has found maximum sustenance and will no longer be deterred. From behind me I heard, "You're finished now, Decker, you know that?" I started downstairs, thinking he must be close behind. At the second-floor landing I glanced up the hallway, flame visible through the smoke. At the final turn in the stairwell there was a fast crashing of steps behind me as if the captain were staggering, or being shoved downward, and as I glanced back I saw why—he had the other bagged snake over his shoulder, gripping it with just one hand. "You're *finished*," he panted, and his voice seemed smaller than ever.

[HEART & ARROW]

In his thirties now, Merrick spends little time at bars, but as he tells his big sister, Laurel, near the end of her fortieth birthday bash, at ten he was a genuine regular.

"What do you mean a *regular?*" Her shrewd blue eyes squint at him through the beige-rimmed glasses he still isn't used to seeing her wear. He looks down, rubbing the blond stubble of a beard that Sheila, his girlfriend back in Toronto, has urged him to grow so he'll look older, more hireable.

"Downstairs," he says. "At Mom and Dad's."

"Well, I don't remember going there. And in high school, believe me, I did the full tour."

"I mean the bar in our basement, Laurel. Our own bar."

"*Oh*—you mean Mom and *Dad's.*"

"That's the place."

She lowers her face—puffy, a bit lined, beautiful—and studies him over the top of her glasses, faint red eyebrows arched, the way their mother used to when she was sober, serious. "Merr. You're not telling me *you*—look, does Sheila know this?—you drank their booze when you were little? You?"

"Hey, that's what I'm telling you." Merrick clinks his glass of rye against her spritzer and forges a coy wink, and his whole manner, he can't help seeing, is lifted from somewhere else—maybe one of those noisy, strobe-lit TV beer ads where a scrum of college jocks flex and guzzle and crack wise along a bar. He can't be sure. But he does know how much he hates the note of glibness that keeps breezing into his voice—the keynote of so much that he reads these days and almost every party he endures. A note he sometimes picks up and sings in tune with, vaguely ashamed the whole time.

Yet at one time his only shame was solitude, exclusion. A time when he'd have given the hand he earns his bread with, marks with—he's a physics teacher now—to sing along with the crowd, to be allowed to, to be let in. But not just any crowd. Contemptuous of his grade-school peers, it was Laurel's tough herd he aspired to, and, somewhere beyond them—through them, really—the grown-up world of his parents' parties.

Guests are shambling out now, halting and awkward, stooping over to embrace Laurel as if she can't get up herself, as if she has aged thirty years with the birthday.

And—it's unsaid but hangs smoke-like in the lamp-lit den—the breakup last month. "Call us if we can do something," a friend says. "I know it'll be fine." After all, it was Laurel's choice and she and Kevin really might "link up again," the boys, in their mid-teens, are pretty stable for their age, and her career in the civil service is going better than she could have planned.

"The black sheep that made good," Merrick toasts her—then, out of character, he kills his rye in one go. Trouble of his own these days. He's broke and even part-time teaching is impossible to find. Funny how things turn out—when they were children it was Merrick who showed all the promise, at least in school.

And now he reminds her of that ironic reversal, to encourage her, he thinks, to cheer her up. Or is it to punish her instead? And what is it that's pushing him to guide her back down that long-demolished stairway into their childhood rec room, the basement bar where he first tried to drown his childhood self and play the hardened, hard-drinking grown-up, while she already seemed set to inherit the only earth that mattered then: a feral frontier of contraband mickeys and smokes, death's head roach clips, classes skipped with a shrug, creatively varied expletives, first lays in junior high. Stoners, they were called, nobody sure if that honorific referred to the state they were always said to be in or to the flooded limestone quarry where they hung out and smoked up and chugged beer and threw themselves naked off the cliffs.

Merrick knows he can't hold back, he has to talk his sister down that basement stairway, and on a particular day. He starts to speak in his best teacher's voice—low, soft, even, implacable—and pours them another round.

That afternoon as usual he had been sitting at one of the high ladderback stools that faced the bar: a kidney-shaped counter of faux marble with a brown buttoned vinyl fronting, set at the head of a low, half-finished rec room. Their father had worked episodically two summers before to finish the basement and then, after a brief bender of late-summer use, both parents had drifted back upstairs, where they had wintered and entertained their friends at the larger bar in the fire-warmed family room. No surprise they'd never returned—the baseboard heaters that Dad installed never quite worked, his light fixtures were few and ill-placed, and even in June the light leaking down through the leaf-choked window wells was dull and sullen, the air stagnant, dank. A Bogart poster and a faded Group of Seven print did little to primp up the cheap panelling behind the bar; in the dimness and stillness the print—of a full moon and stars reflected in a northern lake—had a sombre, ominous quality, as if the water had just smoothed out over a violent drowning. Merrick tried not to look at it. Like Bogart in the poster he brooded into his glass or slouched, cue in hand, at the pool table, where the coloured balls glowed in strange, static constellations, like the solar system in Mr. Leung's model at school.

Merrick liked the muffled gloom of the rec room, especially after school, where the sunlight of the playground and the classroom's crisp lighting always brought into high relief the smallness, the weakness of those in his grade. And himself. Alone at recess he would claw his way up a drainpipe onto the school's flat gravelled roof and stand visoring his eyes, squinting over the subdivision and past the limestone quarry until his gaze was snagged and drawn downward by a fluttering toy-fort flag, a tall smokestack and a soaring, spindly aerial like a high ladder reaching nowhere. Laurel's school. And out beyond it the switchblade glinting of the river, the scarred and furrowed hills.

Laurel was not there, in school. She was hidden away in other, darker basements, doing things that made her parents and her principal and teachers "grey with worry." Without a thought for her family. Unaware, it seemed, of the little brother who still worshipped her and whom she'd happily played with a few years before. (All the toys they had shared were buried in the crawl space under the basement stairs and sometimes during a "binge" in the rec room Merrick would make for that space, lurching and weaving with fierce concentration, and he would take out their old toys and sit playing with them by the light of a bare bulb—a freakish silhouette with his small shoulders dwarfed by his father's fedora.)

He did not get drunk, not very. He did go through the dark cabinets under the sink behind the bar and he shook into jade lacquer bowls the stale, exotic snacks abandoned there—peanuts mummified in mysterious coatings, soggy shrimp wafers, candied ginger. Then, playing bartender, he would set up on the bar a clique of bottles and pour doses of gin or white rum or vodka into shot glasses that gleamed icily in the underground light, as exotic and imposing in their way as the tubes and beakers in Mr. Leung's spotless lab, or the implements and whole rite of Anglican Eucharist, which he had begun taking with his parents each Sunday. Laurel now spurned the sacrament, so he was caught between idols, the adult and the teen, not knowing which to follow, which to betray.

On his first visits to the bar he did not use any mixes, because a man should always take his drink the way his parents did, straight up, but once he became a regular he began groping under the sink for the sticky old bottles of mix forgotten there. He dug out a few half-empty specimens of Pepsi and 7-Up and Canada Dry ginger ale, but they were too flat and anyway they were for kids. The piña colada mix, its gluey cap sporting a skirt of bark shavings, had gone off. But the lime cordial was still good, and dashed with water and a drop of Beefeater gin it made a drink that tasted like lemonade a few days too long in the fridge. Drinkable, barely. His Bloody Marys were better—a jigger of white rum and water diluted with enough grenadine to tint the flooded quarry, he imagined, a bloodshot pink. A spoonful of sugar. He could easily kill two, slumped and rumpled as Bogart at the bar, his father's massive Ray-Bans held on with a pipe cleaner tied around the back.

His parents would not be impressed, he knew. In his gut he knew it and he was always afraid, hearing them up in the family room as suppertime neared, the murmur and slur of their voices strained down through the ceiling—especially his mother's voice, rising with that blurred, abruptly outraged inflection he had come to associate with her second hour of drink. His father's footsteps growing louder, choppier, each time he rose to replenish their glasses. To Merrick it always seemed—especially after his second Bloody Mary, when his guts and small fists unclamped and his veins flooded with sluggish warmth and he thought of himself as "gloriously drunk"—that those footsteps splashed huge shadows across the ceiling, down the panelled walls, over the rec room's fawn linoleum floor. Red shadows. He knew that was ridiculous. He knew that Mr. Leung, who liked and encouraged him in science class, would be disappointed he could think such childish things.

The afternoon Laurel came down to the rec room, Merrick was slouching on the corner stool at the bar. He had on his father's shades and red Shiner's fez and was sucking on an unlit, desiccated cigar, drinking hard, he told himself, to forget. It had been a long day at school and he had picked a fight and lost it and then picked another and won but had not much cared and even Mr. Leung had been curt with him, impatient, it seemed, with his suave familiarities, the way he answered questions as if smoothly responding to the engaging, if imperfect, lecture of a colleague. Shouting now, a crashing of footsteps from close above and big shadows seeming to lunge over the dark walls and ceiling, as had happened before when Laurel came home after staying out all night without calling—but this time she had been gone two nights and the shouting was louder. Hearing feet on the basement stairway instead of the usual shootout of slammed doors, Merrick leapt off the stool and over the bar—the great fez sliding down over his brows—and groped for the bottles he'd lined up, shoving them under the sink with his rancid snacks. And his glass. A Bloody Mary. His third one, for the first time ever a third round, and it had made him awkward and dizzy and he knew he was making too much noise, like that time when another intruder had come down—his mother, her slippers spatting and weaving down the stairs and over the tiles by the crawl space and on into the rec room toward the bar. She hadn't heard any noise Merrick made. With her clumsy movements and her weeping—standing in front of the bar, as if waiting to be served, then shuffling back toward the stairs—she was making too much of her own.

Some day, Merrick hoped, she and Dad would join him at the bar for a round. It would be good to see more of them. But not now. These footfalls were lighter, faster. For a long time he had hoped this would happen, that Laurel would stray down and surprise him in the romantic, reckless, manly act of drinking alone. Hurting himself in private, hurting himself by the glass. And taking it. *Laurel*, he'd wanted to say, *come down to the rec room and I'll fix you a drink—you don't need to stay out late with those friends of yours.* But he'd been afraid she might laugh at him, or disbelieve him, or even turn him in to their parents. But if she just *happened* on him, how different things would seem. *Merry, I had no idea you were so cool . . . shit, you don't have to sit here all alone if you don't want.*

But he'd hidden himself and the bottles and it was too late to present the unforgettable image he'd pictured. Time only for this: grip the last of his Bloody Mary and leap up behind the bar to toast her, let her see him as he was, a man. He caught a glimpse of her and froze. He ducked down. Like their mother she was crying but in a different way—with a terrifying, sobbing urgency, her red curls shaking over her freckled face, eyes bruised with smeared mascara.

She turned and walked stiffly toward the crawl space and Merrick had to crane his head around the edge of the bar to watch her open the low door, kneel down, squeeze in. He couldn't guess what she might want in there among the jumbled remnants of their childhood, dolls and stuffed animals and board games and science kits and hockey cards and Lego. He drained his drink. The pounding in his head seemed to come from elsewhere, as if his parents, drunk again, were stumbling around upstairs in search of the drinks they had set down somewhere and forgotten. Laurel crawled backward out of the dark space and punched the door shut, her old pink skipping rope clenched in her fist.

She was no longer crying. Her face was grey. She stood on tiptoe and struggled to knot one end of the rope to the brass hook screwed into the ceiling for a spider plant that had died in the chilly dimness and been removed. Laurel moved toward the bar. Merrick pulled in his head. The grating of a stool being dragged away over the linoleum, then a faint wet sob, more a hiccup. He peered out again. Laurel was trying to balance her bare feet on the middle rung of the stool base as she stood wobbling, the seat's edge crimping the backs of her bare thighs, her arms raised, hands fumbling with the rope. Merrick felt choked as if by the tie he liked to wear to church Sunday mornings but could never quite knot, so that his father, surly, eyes sunken small and red, had to be summoned to help.

Summon him now, he thought. Both of them.

But Laurel pulled back, settled on the stool, wept weakly, and Merrick let out his breath, yet he was still afraid of startling her, so he waited—a minute, two minutes—the time seeming to stretch into hours, the way a ten-foot drop will deepen to a hundred when you're trying to do it—jump—and he saw himself back in the brutal sunlight up on the edge of the quarry where his sister and her gang always went. A month earlier he had followed them up to the edge, yet again, telling himself it was to watch over Laurel in secret, but really hoping they would notice him and ask him over for a drink. Hunched, sunglassed and sweating in the tall grass, he'd spied her and the others sprawling in the unseasonably warm sun on the clifftop, a transistor radio and a two-four of Red Cap in the gravel among them. The Band was playing "Stage Fright." Some of the stoners dozed and sunbathed. Laurel and her wiry boyfriend, who had a full tan although it was just May, sat face to face, legs pretzeled together on an open sleeping bag, sharing a smoke and a beer, Laurel gently reaching her hands along the boy's sideburned face and inching up the bandana wreathed hippie-style around his long straight hair. Kissing his open lips. Merrick's face scalding as the boy's brown hand slipped into Laurel's bikini top.

One of the stoners, skinny chest tattooed, sat up in mock umbrage, tore off his mirrored John Lennon shades and in what Merrick knew to be a parody of their principal's Scottish accent (Laurel often mocked him at home) told them to mind their deportment or they would be passing the whole night in detention. And another boy, working off a beer cap with the blade of his pocketknife, said, "They just need a cool dip."

They were all up now, ready to throw Laurel and her boyfriend over the edge, but the two of them raised their hands in genial surrender and got up, stretching like lean, limber animals and daring each other to go first. When the tattooed boy with the granny shades, his bangs so long they seemed to part around his sharp nose, bent and clinched the boyfriend around the waist as if to trundle him over, Laurel coolly stripped off her bikini and with a whoop sped away toward the edge. In motion that way—naked, running—she was a stranger to Merrick, without a face or a name. As she moved he was flushed and anxious and then, as she leapt out into space, he gasped *Laurel.* His last glimpse of her was a starburst of long red curls splayed out by the momentum of her jump.

The boyfriend ran to the edge, looked down, waved. Merrick hadn't heard the splash. Now the boyfriend turned from the cliff and peeled off his tight cut-offs, revealing dense black pubic hair and a long, half-swollen penis—larger, Merrick realized with a shock, than his father's, glimpsed in the bath.

After the boyfriend's jump, Merrick stumbled out of the grass.

"Who's the kid with the monster shades?" a girl asked.

"Where?" said the tattooed boy.

Merrick couldn't see the tattoo clearly. He took off his sunglasses.

"Oh, fuck, it's Laurel's kid brother again."

"Tell him to beat it," the girl said.

"She can do it herself," the tattooed boy said, gesturing with his bottle at the cliff, where Laurel was just appearing, head and shoulders and small high breasts seeming to levitate over the precipice. She must have been climbing a steep path. Her bare skin still dripped, glowed with the freezing water, the ice just a few weeks gone. The tattooed boy whistled and Laurel blushed from the breasts up and rolled her eyes and flitted over to her things and dressed with great speed, as if the bikini could warm her.

"Your kid brother."

Laurel, fumbling behind her back, looked up with smudged, startled eyes and frowned hard, then blushed again. "What are you doing here, Merrick?"

"Don't know," he mumbled. Then he lied: "Came to jump, I guess."

"Don't be an idiot," the other girl said.

"We'd be in it deep," the tattooed boy said, "if he got hurt."

Laurel stared at Merrick. She shook her head and looked skyward, long-sufferingly, the way she always did with their parents, then fastened her gaze on the clifftop. After a moment she shrugged, or maybe shuddered, and made a lopsided smile. "If he really wants to, he can try."

"We'd be in deep shit."

"Kid can hardly walk, Laur. He's like hardly out of diapers."

"Shut up, Cathy," Laurel said. "Just shut the fuck up, okay?"

"Must be a hundred feet down," the tattooed boy said and cocked an eyebrow over one mirrored lens, as if Merrick were an idiot incapable of decoding such grade-school irony.

The boyfriend appeared on the lip of the cliff, wet headband high on his forehead, sinewy torso clenched up and shaking, his penis retracted now, puny as a child's.

"That your kid brother again, Laur?"

"I can do it," Merrick said, and spat dryly. "No shit. I can."

Someone gave a hoot of derision or excitement and the radio's volume shot up: The Who, "I Can See for Miles."

Laurel, still knotting her brow, reached out her hand. "Okay, Merr, come on. Don't listen to those guys. It's fun, I'll show you."

And she did. She led him to the precipice and she told him what to do and she told him again, then again, with dwindling patience, as he stood there for a full hour, stripped to his jockey shorts, sweating and trembling, eyes trained on his watch or on his lily feet or the scared, bloodless bump of his cock in the white jockey shorts, to avoid seeing the water far below as his big chance ticked away and the stoners sauntered up beside him and teased or encouraged him and one after another, with some hesitation, leapt. Laurel said it was just forty feet to the water, tops, all you had to do was tuck in your arms and go straight down, but to Merrick the drop seemed endless, sickening as that film he had seen at school: the camera in a jet fighter skimming low and fast over the desert toward the edge of the Grand Canyon, till the drop shudders into view and in a flash the earth's floor shears away and the abyss explodes under you and your breath is gone, your guts, you're plummeting till the life-cord jerks taut and your parachute hangs you in mid-air—a jolt like the slap on a newborn's back—and you breathe. Even the toughest of Laurel's gang were a bit scared. It took most of them a minute or two, and two or three chugs of beer, to muster the courage for each jump, and when they did jump they would gangle and windmill their arms like third graders on a trampoline—though once they surfaced they were themselves again, cured, aged, by the waters, the way liquor could age you, absolve you of childhood—the tattooed boy coolly tossing his head to flick the wet bangs from his eyes.

After an hour they went back to their beer and left Merrick on the edge of the cliff, teeth rattling, loose limestone shards stabbing at his soles. In the distance past the city the river was a long, quivering blade carving up the sandbars, and beyond it the hills seemed to fold and crumple under waves of rising heat. Down on the water Merrick's shadow looked scrawny. It seemed to move like an hour hand as the sun burning his neck and shoulders crossed the sky behind him and began to fall. But if Merrick couldn't jump, he could not back away either, though Laurel, feet slung over the edge where she sat digging red fingernails into a beer label, was now trying to talk him out of it, telling him it was cool, the cliff was bigger for him than it was for them 'cause he was still so small, right? Shit, he was the brain on relativity.

Her brow and mouth began to pucker, harden. She grabbed their father's sunglasses—they were hooked over her bikini top between her breasts—and stuck them on. He choked back a welling in his throat. For a few years they had hardly exchanged a word and now she was making this overture, offering him this chance, and he knew he could not shame them both and let her down.

But he could not jump.

Laurel got up and tilted her beer back and drained it and hurled the bottle out across the quarry. It seemed to fall for a long time. "Maybe you should be heading home, kid." And as he nodded gravely and half turned, realizing his last chance was squandered, a stone flipped, jabbing his heel, and he lost balance, lurched forward and knew he was falling and that knowledge braced him with a kind of helpless courage. Laurel reached out to help him but he launched with his feet, arms flapping, and he was airborne—motionless it seemed—then gravity was roaring up through his bowels and belly and throat and the dark circle of the water was surging up at him like a maw. He whipped his arms for balance and kicked at the air but at the last moment he wobbled off-kilter, yelled and smacked the water at an angle not quite belly flat but bad enough, and when the roaring, the wild kaleidoscope of ice-green fragments, had wound down to a stillness, the sun's heat was on his face and eyelids and from high above came the mewing of a gull. Lips were being pressed to his, breath flowed into him in waves. He coughed wetly and heard Laurel close behind him, panting, then something eclipsed the sun and he opened his eyes: the tattooed boy's granny shades goggled down through the long, bracketing wings of hair, his sunken chest a few inches away as he tried to nurse Merrick with a bottle of beer. Drinking the warm beer, Merrick eyed his chest tattoo: a conventional pierced, bleeding-heart design, except the thin black arrow was tipped at both ends.

"You all right? Fuck, kid, that was some belly flop. You cool?"

He nodded. Because he'd done it. Even if Laurel, they told him, had had to dive in and fish him out because he was too shocked by the impact and the cold to swim. And later as she walked him home she'd actually let him know how proud she was—maybe in part, he guessed, so he wouldn't tell their mother what had happened, how he'd wrenched his neck and ankle and lost his watch and nearly drowned. As if he would tell. "At first I thought you just slipped, then I realized you were really jumping. But it looked so strange. Like there was somebody behind you pushing you and you were trying not to go off the edge, but this invisible thing was pushing you. And the way your arms were flapping! Fuck, Merr, I'm sorry to be . . . I'm glad you're all right." As she draped a sunburned arm around his shoulders (maybe less in sibling solidarity than to help him walk), he felt a grin surge up inside him and burst into daylight like a man surfacing from far below after a perfect dive, arms raised, lungs inhaling the air in rapture and relief.

But that hour turned out to be an interlude, a singularity, not a fresh start, and in the weeks that followed he saw Laurel less than ever before. As if that day had meant little to her. As if the ripples caused by his jump—which to him had seemed seismic, he being the first in his school to do it—were for her soon overwhelmed by the churnings of some greater storm.

When she leapt off the barstool it seemed some invisible thing had shoved her, because the set of her face and body and even the last twitch before the fall all seemed to be resisting it—yet she did fall, and when the short noose jerked her with a tight, shuddering bounce, her legs started scissoring, a child in a tantrum, trying to kick away the stool or to climb back on. The stool toppled over. There was an echoing crash upstairs. Laurel's hands clutched spastically at the pink rope tightening around her neck. Her pale face reddened, her eyes bulged, the trembling jump rope strained to its limit.

For seconds he had been frozen like up on the precipice but now, again, something shoved him out of the grip of fear, or whatever it was that held him. He was halfway to her, calling "Laurel, Laurel, please!" when he realized the rope was still stretching, like a piece of licorice pulled apart, his sister slowly descending to the floor.

The glass slipped from his hand and smashed at his

feet. Their mother was yelling from the head of the stairs. Laurel was lighting on her toes, clawing at the rope still squeezing her neck, glaring as he threw himself at her and gripped her around the belly to lift her and ease the choking, and a vision came of the two of them in the quarry, underwater, Laurel buoying him up through tunnels of turquoise light until they breached in a shock of sunlight and spray, he gulped at the air, she towed him coughing back to shore . . . Merrick heard her gasp. He looked up and she was scowling down as if to say, *Let go of me, you moron, get this fucking jump rope off my neck.*

Their mother loomed before them, a drink in one hand, pawing at her glasses with the other as if to clear a lens and discredit this hellish scene: her delinquent daughter half hanged beside the shattered barstool and her sunglassed ten-year-old drunk, cut open, kneeling in glass like shards of ice, as if he'd just hauled her up out of a hole in the river.

The last guests are gone and Merrick and Laurel clean up. She's quiet now, tired, it seems, and sad. Partly it's Kevin. For fifteen years he has been a solid part of their small galaxy of family and friends, a satellite of stable orbit, and now abruptly his orbit has changed and carried him off in a way that violates all the old logic, old laws.

Merrick is thinking of things in this way because of his own teaching and because talk of that day at the quarry has reminded him of something the whole school believed then. Mr. Leung notwithstanding, it was a well-known fact that the quarry had been formed thousands of years before by a meteorite: a great flaming boulder billowing clouds of smoke had shrieked down through the atmosphere and stamped itself into the limestone, leaving behind a crater, scorched cliffs, a deep glacial-green socket of water that had spilled in from the river two miles off.

"But you must have known it wasn't true before the rest of us," Laurel tells him, looking drawn and cross in the kitchen's guttering fluorescent light. Almost three a.m. They stand over the sink washing up, the clack of glass and the slopping of water a bland, comforting counterpoint to the hard talk they've been having. "I mean, you always were a smart kid for your age. Always in such a hurry to grow up."

"Sure," he says, trying to gauge her tone, "so I knew it wasn't a meteorite. Fine. I knew that and a lot more. But where did it get me? All those facts, I mean. The *hurry*." He looks down into the ticking suds, embarrassed.

Her voice softens a little. "Well, you'll find something soon, I'm sure you will. And Sheila's work's secure, I'll bet."

"No shortage of work these days for addiction counsellors."

"Anyway, it's a recession. You said yourself that a lot of the colleges—"

"I'm doing fine," he says. "Listen, I'm sorry."

"It's three in the morning, you don't usually drink, you're entitled to feel a bit sorry for yourself." She doesn't sound convinced.

"Not just that. I mean for bringing up what happened. But I've been . . . you can see I've been mulling it over for years and I guess . . ."

"It's all right." She shoves her towel-wrapped fingers into the last glass to swab it dry. "I just wish we remembered things the same. I remember a bit of the hospital after, and the shrinks, and you and Dad coming to visit—you brought me adult books every time, remember? Instead of magazines? But going down to the basement, the rope—I haven't blocked any of that out, Merrick, it's just clearer all the time." She swabs harder now, insistent, the glass getting streaked and cloudy with specks of lint. "And you weren't there, Merrick. You really were not. You think I could have forgotten that?"

She grinds the glass into the crammed dish rack.

"Fuck, none of you were ever there, that was the whole problem."

"Laurel."

"You came down with Mom at the end. Just when I was pulling it off. You both just . . . stood there, gawking, then she screamed and ran over and she held me. For once in her fucking life."

"But I was there the whole time—I was right there! People remember things differently when—"

"They remember things *wrong*," she cries with something of her old fire, and behind her new glasses her eyes roll like a teenager's.

"Laurel, listen."

"And I *was* lying when I said I knew you'd jumped, not slipped. On the cliff. You're grown up now, you can handle it. It's a small thing anyway. But I knew you slipped all along, I just wanted to make you feel better."

He twists out the stopper and the sink gives a throttled gargling and empties faster than any sink he's ever seen. A spattered, sudsy jumble of cutlery breaks surface, bones on the floor of a drained lake. (When he was in high school a construction firm had finally drained the quarry, revealing oil drums, dumpsters, gutted TVs, bicycles, several cars, thousands of beer bottles and the weed-green skeleton of an unknown man. They had built a large shopping mall over the top, at ground level, and turned the pit beneath it into an underground car park, where Merrick, in town last spring for an unsuccessful interview, parked and bought flowers for his parents' graves.)

"Mine's always plugged," he says, putting his watch back on.

"What?"

"My sink."

After a few seconds she turns to him, her glasses fogged over.

"I'm sorry I said those things. I didn't mean it, Merr, I'm sorry, I'm just so wiped out these days, and . . ."

"Forget it."

"The kids tell me I'm biting everyone's head off."

Briskly, lightly, so as not to embarrass her, he sets his hands on her stooped shoulders and kisses the dulled freckles on her cheek. The hair at her temples, once fire-coloured, has cooled to ashen. Or is that tempered to steel? She's wearing their mother's old Sunday earrings, small crosses of white gold.

"Laurel?" He speaks softly, hugs her and rubs her bowed back as it begins to quiver, then shake. "It's all right, Laur. Go ahead, I don't mind. Go get some rest." She pulls her head back from his shoulder and he can see her face: she's laughing, actually, although her eyes are full.

"It did look so damn funny when you went off, you know. With that stupid hat on your head and those big sunglasses."

He doesn't remember a hat.

As Merrick puts the last of the good glasses away in their box—checking each by raising it to the light, as if focusing a small scope on a heavenly body—he notices the set is incomplete, two missing, and he starts up the narrow hallway toward the living room to find them. A ragged, somehow elderly snoring already ripples from Laurel's room. He pauses, socks aglow, by the yawning full-moon nightlight between his nephews' doors and thinks of Sheila, how good it will be to get back to their place in Toronto tomorrow night and make love and sleep beside her again and how bad it will be the next day when they start fighting again about family, how she wants one urgently and he's still afraid. "There's no work out there," he'll say again, though they both know that's not really it. And she'll tell him again in her best counsellor's voice that a fear of children is a fear of growing up.

Maybe the glasses are in one of the boy's rooms, but he won't stumble in and wake them the way his own parents used to, searching for their lost drinks how many years ago. Like Laurel he *is* different from them, he has learned something; there is, he believes, some progress in time. He'll go on up the hall into the living room and check there, then out the sliding doors into the cool yard the way his parents did more and more in their last years, searching. He still has occasional dreams of them shuffling like sleepwalkers, miles out from the house and the city and years beyond all houses, over dunes along the moonlit beach, wading out to vanish at a bend in the river, or silhouetted, hand in hand, on the cliffs above the drop.

[JOURNEYMEN]

Cutler was running alone, as he preferred to run these days, on the gorgeous, lethally hilly trail he called the Monster. He'd named it after a challenging roller-coaster he'd ridden years before with his younger child, Mattie. The boy, six years old, had been speechless with delighted terror, his mouth gaping, eyes squinted, auburn ringlets blown back almost straight as he shrank into Cutler's ribcage and Cutler held him tighter by the second—partly a response to his own vertigo and fear.

The Monster was Cutler's favourite trail and one that Mattie, in his mid to late teens, had often run with him. An adolescent boy's fountain of fresh hormones can do as much to strengthen him as training can, and so Mattie had gained ground on Cutler in rapid, regular spikes of improvement, until he was the faster—though never by very much. The boy hadn't inherited Cutler's exceptional talent. He hadn't been deeded Cutler's drive, either, and on the whole Cutler thought that a very good thing. A sweet kid, adored by girls from kindergarten until college, protected by his male friends, he took after his gentle, dreamy mother, with her wide-set grey eyes and slow, unguarded smiles that seemed to hint at some private wisdom unavailable to the manic outer world. So as the boy's third-, fourth- or fifth-place ribbons accumulated, he'd accepted their verdict in his usual easy-natured way: he would never be more than a respectable club or varsity athlete. This equanimity was another thing Cutler had loved about him. It's a myth, he thought, that competitive parents all want their children to take after them and then grow up to exceed them, to summit the Alp-like ambitions the parents themselves never quite attained. The last thing Cutler had wanted was to see Mattie and his older sister, Esme, driving themselves as he'd once driven himself.

The erosive current of time and circumstance had worn down his own urge to perfect and prevail, athletically, socially, professionally; Cutler had simplified into a more or less peaceful man. Unfortunately Esme was displaying most of her father's former symptoms (minus, thank God, the self-destructiveness). Since toddlerhood she'd done so. She was now an economics professor at Cornell, and Grace and Cutler saw her only in the summer and at Christmas. She'd married a lawyer, a self-proclaimed libertarian (he was always proclaiming it) who, despite having graduated in Canada from government-subsidized schools into a profession where he was grossing over two hundred thousand a year, saw personal taxation as institutionalized piracy, a sort of fiscal terrorism inflicted by the lazy and covetous on the successful. Grace made artful dinnertime detours around Trevor's positions, but Cutler—an exception to the general rule that men grow less progressive with age—was apt to crash into them head-on. And hours later Grace, in bed beside him, her ear on his collarbone and her soft white hair fanned out on his chest, would whisper, "He's our *son* now, Cutler, you need to try harder." And he would nod and breathe and slowly exhale and for Grace's sake he would not burst out, "Our *son*? Grace, Grace! Mattie was our only son."

Cutler was not surprised to be feeling good on the trail, despite his rotten day in the clinic. He'd been running for forty years and had long since quit trying to detect correlations between how he felt during the day and his running performance at the end of it. Some of his best runs had come on afternoons when he'd had to choose between lugging his aching limbs out onto the trail or returning to bed for a nap. In his twenties, at university and medical school, aiming for Olympic glory and falling not far short, the chief problem had been almost daily, crushing hangovers. In his thirties—too late for the sake of his Olympic goals—he'd quit drinking and married and then the marriage itself had become the stressor. Though he'd been drawn to Grace Holland's calm, almost tranquillized demeanour, once legally bound to it he'd panicked, flailed about, as if compelled to heave from a tossing lifeboat the very ballast that keeps it from tipping. He guessed now that those had been the death throes of his old self. They went on for an operatically long time, Grace waiting him out with a quiet, cast-iron stubbornness. Over a stretch of some years, he spent many nights alone on the pullout in his study, reading professional journals or running magazines and hearing his daughter sleeping in the next room. In retrospect, even her unconscious breathing had a rushed and restless quality, as though she was always champing for tomorrow to arrive.

By Cutler's forties the marriage had settled, its molten materials cooled and stabilized. They had the children and a house and his clinical office on the edge of Wakefield, at the gateway to his beloved trails. By that point, any day-end fatigue he experienced had more to do with mid-life's interlocking demands, especially those of his thriving practice as a sports doctor combined with his volunteer coaching (and his family—but that went without saying). Still, at five p.m. he almost always chose the trails instead of his office couch.

In his mid-fifties he began spending less time at the clinic. He and Grace, who'd taken early retirement from her middle-school teaching job, started going on actual holidays, an indulgence he'd once been too focused and fidgety to enjoy. Now, if he was weary at four thirty or five p.m., he was tempted to assign it not to stress but to age, the way his friends did. In fact, though, he was still running strongly and seldom missed a day, despite having suffered some minor attrition of the usual connective tissues, as well as a loss of pliancy and spring-loading in the Achilles and calf caused by years of wearing shoes with raised heels, the great biomechanical blunder of the Western world, he now saw. Cutler was fifty-eight—a ripe age for that first culling, through stroke, heart disease, or cancer, of a substantial minority of his demographic—but age wasn't the real problem. The problem was the sadness that would hemorrhage through him at times, generally toward day's end and especially in the autumn, when the prima donna leaves of the Gatineau hills showcased their dying in rich yellows, ambers, reds.

They'd lost Mattie in November, four years before, and now all the weeks from the equinox until Christmas were touched and tainted with the loss. The boy had been running at dusk in Montreal, a city he was in love with and where he lived with his fiancée, Elise, who had not been running with him that day, thank God. At a busy intersection near Parc Mont Royal, a Humvee bearing the logo of a classic rock radio station had turned right blindly, its driver chatting on a cellphone, and hurled Mattie out of the crosswalk into the side of a bus shelter. It was as if the kid had been thrown by a train, according to a witness quoted in one news report that Cutler wished he had never read—though of course, being Cutler, he had read and clipped or printed them all and filed them away with his old compulsive diligence.

Some friends were surprised that, after the way his son had been killed, Cutler still ran. He would explain that the running made him feel closer to Mattie. It was another way he chose to remember the boy—and, despite his friends' advice, he felt sure there could never be too much remembering. Too much *grieving*, maybe, but grief and remembrance were not the same thing. Mattie, too, had loved these woods; rerunning their routes now, through the dense plexus of the trails, was like retracing neural pathways where memories of the boy were inerasably stored.

What he didn't tell his friends was that he *had* to keep running—that more than ever he was a junkie hooked on the body's hormonal narcotics, the serotonin, the endorphins, the THC-like compounds secreted through exercise. Those substances had not been enough to keep him from falling off the wagon after the funeral, but the running did help him quit again, after a full year of renewed drinking.

Cutler sped into one of his favourite turns, a ninety-degree elbow through a stand of hemlocks. Their cool citrusy scent—a sharp change from the burnt, toasty odour of fallen hardwood leaves—cleared his head. Years' worth of needles were compressed level and firm underfoot. He leaned in on the turn like a skater. It felt good as always. Running could be like dance, like play, once you didn't have to fret about the mechanics or entry-level fatigue.

He rounded the corner and a view opened ahead and below: the trail widening as it fell away through a stand of mature sugar maples. Come March, stripped to the bone, they would be tapped, spiled and slung with aluminum sap pails; for now, the October sun electrified their dense foliage. The downhill stretch here was stony, runnelled with washouts, but from the base of the grade ran a smooth, flat straightaway—a perfect sprinter's lane—to an unrailed wooden bridge over a creek.

Cutler was halfway down the slope when he noticed two things at once: at the base of the hill, a couple with a toddler were emerging from the sugar wood onto the trail, while from behind Cutler came the sound of what must be a mountain bike thumping over the first few ruts as it began the descent. The family spread across the trail below, parents on the outside, the child between them holding their hands and dawdling, setting the pace. From behind Cutler the aggressive slamming bore down while he himself gained on the trio. Normally by now he would have coughed or kicked a stone aside to alert them of his near-silent approach, but he figured they must hear the cyclist. In his gut a premonitory flitter, which was odd—he'd often negotiated little rush hours of walkers, runners and cyclists, jaunty hikers with ski poles, overly sociable dogs. Somehow this felt different. The cyclist was closing fast and the family hardly moving. Cutler's brain computed likely conjunctions. He glanced back—a risky measure while trotting downhill over loose washboard—and got a flash of the cyclist a few metres back, half-braking now, the chassis of his bike thudding over the ruts as he steered wide. A weight-room physique sealed into one of those space-age black bodysuits, wraparound sunglasses like heat shields, a road racer's comet-shaped helmet. Clenched lips set off with fashionable stubble.

Cutler, slowing, looked forward again, the family close in front of him, the toddler oblivious, mother and father glancing back at last, heads swivelling in unison. Cutler wasn't sure which way to move—which way the family would move—and at the same time from some inner recess sprang a fierce aversion to moving, anger at the cyclist's reckless impatience, the overstated physique, the exhibitionistic, high-end gear (Cutler's stuff hadn't changed since the '70s: anonymous cotton shorts, T-shirts, hooded sweatshirts). This trail was for walkers and runners as well as cyclists. The parents were exchanging mixed signals, converging to sandwich the child and then recoiling, then lurching leftward with the child between them, and Cutler was about to move left as well when the cyclist snarled, "Fuck, man, trail, *trail!*" The voice was wrong for the face and the body, as most voices are. Instead of a husky, territorial bass it was nasal and high, peevish, almost effete. Cutler edged left, just barely, and the cyclist, pedalling to regain speed, jolted past him to the right, not quite off the trail. Cutler flung him a look. The man stared straight ahead through his sunglasses, as if Cutler were now invisible, eliminated by his words. There was no physical contact but Cutler felt the draft of the man's passing and smelled the fresh oil on his derailleur, clean sweat in his gear. His watch looked as complex as a smartphone. As his tires gripped the hard-packed straightaway and sped off, a birdshot of dirt and bits of gravel churned up by the tires' deep grooves spattered Cutler's legs. It was nothing much—like passing through a constellation of mayflies while you run on the first warm evening of spring—and maybe that would have been the end of it, but at that very instant the man called back in a jeering voice, "Dude, if you're too slow for the traffic . . ."

Maybe he'd meant to conclude *you should just stay home* but was saving himself the breath. By "too slow" Cutler assumed he meant "too old." Above all, though, there was that "dude." Cutler could have chosen to see it as a compliment by default—as if, despite Cutler's greying hair and expanding bald patch, the man had somehow taken him for a peer. Instead, the word's sneering chumminess seemed to sharpen and barb the taunt.

"Well, *he's* in a hurry, isn't he?" the young mother called in a voice loud enough to include the passing Cutler, along with her partner and child, though probably not the receding cyclist. Her censure of the man seemed mild, philosophical. Cutler, starting to speed up on an aftersurge of adrenaline, glanced back over his shoulder, raised a hand and nodded once, as if to say, *So everyone's okay, then?* The mother was a light-skinned South Asian, the father older, heavy, with freckled pink skin and a squashed-looking face. As he met Cutler's gaze, Cutler realized the man was as angry at *him* as at the cyclist.

The cyclist seemed to be slowing now, gliding over the small bridge, while Cutler was still accelerating, as if he really thought he could catch him. True, if the man stopped for maintenance up ahead, or took enough time at the trailhead parking lot racking his bike onto the roof of his vehicle (Cutler imagined a Jeep or some kind of SUV), he might get to have a word with him. Long odds. The guy didn't seem the type to take his time doing anything. He'd brought the brusque urgency of the city—or the age itself, gridlocked in perpetual rush hour—into these woods where Cutler was still trying to hide out from time.

Cutler longed to slow time, even halt and force it backward through some quantum wormhole—a feat actually achievable in certain early morning dreams from which he always woke in tears. After the boy's death the world had not just gone on with its business, indifferently, but also seemed to accelerate away from Grace and Cutler and leave them behind, huddled together, crushed and redundant, at the graveside. He did wonder if what he perceived as the world's new surliness and haste was an illusion born of the contrasting stillness and silence of grief. Or was it just his age?

Grace didn't tease him about getting old physically—they were lovers as active, he guessed, as many thirty-year-olds, even if for a year after the death they had both wondered if sex was finished for them. She meant old mentally, in his complaints about the age's steroidal vulgarity.

He reached the bridge and loped across, feeling the give and spring-back of the planks, like on the two-hundred-metre indoor track at the CNE grounds back in the '70s when he was training for Montreal. He couldn't enjoy the sensation this time. The cyclist was out of view beyond the next bend in the trail. By now, in fact, the guy might be half finished the tough set of switchbacks zippering up out of the valley. Cutler, starting to feel the pace in his lungs, eased off. Still, he was in good form today, fluent, light-limbed, and he would finish his route at a decent speed, burn off this mainline hit of cortisol and calm himself down.

Cutler had been a true amateur in the '70s, the age of "shamateurs" along with those East European guinea pigs, many now dead but at the time undefeatably amped up on synthetic androgens and other chemical jelly beans. He too had been obsessive—no athlete succeeding at a national level could be anything less—but he hadn't believed in winning at any price, if that price included shooting up, lying and cheating. (As if to be extra fair, he'd actually *handicapped* himself with a performance-reducing substance, alcohol.) Still, maybe it was true, what one recent patient had confided.

A college hurdler leaning toward steroids, he'd told Cutler that being a "good loser"—he framed the term with derisively twitching fingers—was no longer an option; it was naive to think anyone could compete at the highest level now without chemicals.

Cutler rounded the bend and saw movement ahead and above: the cyclist was two-thirds of the way up the hill, moving slowly around the first of four tight switchbacks at the toughest part. Of course he wouldn't be at the top yet—Cutler had forgotten how steep the grade became halfway up, how much it would slow a cyclist, even in lowest gear. Cutler accelerated into the base of the hill. He felt a sort of hunterly excitement, made a fresh projection of possible conjunctions. He might be able to beat the guy to the top. Leaning into the slope, he kept his steps light and short and worked his arms, almost silent.

The cyclist was steering around the second-last hairpin when Cutler caught him. Instead of trying to get around him—the trail too narrow here—he cut up across the hairpin, almost sliding back on the loose stuff that shot out from under his scrambling treads. Without glancing at the cyclist, who seemed startled, he rejoined the trail—now levelling out, straightening, widening—and pushed for the top. Stay relaxed, make it look easy, like a jog, that was the secret, though it wasn't easy, not after a forty-metre hill, Cutler's legs breaking down on this short final pitch.

Don't look back. Never look back.

Just before Cutler crested the hill, the cyclist came breezing alongside, his big speed-skater thighs pumping fast in shiny tights. The clean, efficient hum of his machine, in lowest gear. As the grade lessened, then flattened, he cruised away up the trail without a glance back and it struck Cutler that the guy had only been slow on the hill before because he'd chosen to stay in higher gear, to work his legs. Of course. It was absurd to think a fifty-eight-year-old, drug-free runner, however strong, could outpace a man half his age on a well-tuned machine. Yet Cutler, however foolish, was not slowing down. He had to keep the rider in sight—and for now it was possible, the trail's next leg running straight as a baseline road for half a kilometre. Naturally the cyclist was opening a gap, though not as fast as either he or Cutler might have expected; the man's wide torso swayed violently as he rode, a kind of seated swagger that Cutler knew was slowing him down. Maybe he was tired from a long workout. Or he wasn't such an athlete after all. A grandstander with toy muscles and a cartoon mascot's gritted teeth.

Cutler sped up. At the end of this stretch, as he knew well but the cyclist might not, the trail descended again into the gully of another creek. It snaked tightly down through cedars and firs and there the cyclist would definitely have to slow. Cutler would catch him before he got to the bottom. Across that creek, a mirror slope climbed fifty metres—Mattie had named it the Reaper, after some lethal entity in one of his video games—and even in lowest gear a cyclist would have to stick to the switchbacks. If Cutler could run straight up, off-trail, he could put even more distance between them.

In his ear, Grace's drowsy, droll voice—his internalized good sense, his moral positioning system—remarked that when he wasn't playing the irascible old crank he was making like a child. Racing some grade-school rival home through the woods. Well, so be it. Even these days (all right, especially these days), when he came upon another runner or heard one behind him, he automatically, helplessly sped up. It was just something that runners of a certain calibre and competitive background did, he told himself, though at times he caught inklings of a deeper truth: that he ran these days in a state of quiet fury, never far from his grief.

He started down the hairpin descent almost faster than was safe. He couldn't see the cyclist below through the trees but could hear him crunching over the gravel stretch where Parks Canada had rebuilt a washed-out hairpin. That would be halfway down, more or less. Cutler loved zipping down this bit of trail, slaloming the tight corners. All his running life he'd preferred cross-country to track because of such pleasures, leaning into banked turns as if riding motocross, feeling the gears shift in the brain's intuitive transmission as contours change underfoot, new scenery always unfurling, crossing winter fields of unmarked powder or barefooting beaches and the night-cool, velveteen greens of golf courses.

His love of cross-country had probably cost him in the end. By 1974, when Cutler was twenty-two and on a winning streak, his coach had begged him to start training more on the road and especially on the track, the track, the track. Cross-country was just strength-work. The *season* was varsity track in winter and spring, club and nationals come summer. But he couldn't stay off the trails. The grinding track intervals he added to his routine deepened his allergy. "Look," he said—or remembered saying—"if I spend the next five years running around a quarter-mile track and fail, I'm nothing and I've gone nowhere. If I spend those years out in the woods, I might still be no one but at least I've *been* somewhere." His coach pointed out correctly that champions didn't hedge their bets—and that Cutler needed to stop drinking if he was going to get really serious.

But he was serious, he was ranked, and in the best race of his life—the '75 World Cross-Country championship in Morocco—he was the top Canadian, finishing twenty-first in a large field. This was before the East African onslaught of the '80s and '90s changed everything; still, the performance impressed many and Cutler seemed a genuine hope for the Montreal Olympics. But at the Canadian trials for the 10,000 he got boxed in and tripped heavily and he had to qualify in the 5,000 instead. He made it, but in the opening Olympic heat, scared yet elated, soaring on adrenaline, he started too fast, led the field for four laps and by midrace was struggling. The 5,000 was not his event and the track was not his element. The media didn't mention those factors and Cutler, watching a replay of the heat a few days later, was stung by their offhand dismissal of his effort. The commentators—who like most North American sportscasters knew little more about track and field than they knew about cricket or canoe-polo—described Cutler Connell as "either out of shape or out of his league." They didn't understand what a world-class 5,000-metre race meant: a three-mile-plus sprint. Neither commentator could have run the length of a city block at the pace he averaged for those thirteen minutes and fifty-eight seconds.

He caught the cyclist just before the bottom of the hill. This time he surprised him not at the moment of passing but seconds before, since downhill steps, however light, are never silent, especially over gravel. The man glanced up, his sunglasses hiding the look in his eyes but his black eyebrows twitching up over the rims. This time Cutler had to pass him on the outside of the last hairpin and he managed it neatly, twisting his torso to squeeze past the right handlebar with a gruff, significant, "Pardon me."

The gully floor was narrow and sunless, carved out by a bouillon-coloured creek whose channel ferried a glowing flotilla of oak, beech and maple leaves southward to the Ottawa. As Cutler crossed another small bridge—weathered, moss-grown, it seemed more a process of nature than an amendment of it—the cyclist pumped past him, as expected, working hard, bunched over his handlebars like a kid speeding on a tricycle. But now the Reaper. Cutler charged into it, to the left of the zigzag trail, while the cyclist swung into the first switchback, downshifting and pedaling fast—no more trace of pretence now, fully committed to the race. So was Cutler, yet now he wondered if he'd miscalculated—whether the slope was too steep to run up off-trail, the surface too crumbly. He dug with his arms like a sprinter. By halfway up he was leaden, lactic, but here the grade eased off ten degrees and he slowed and glanced down and back: the cyclist was well behind him, stitching his way up the hairpins. Cutler drove himself on, each exhalation a grunt of pain. This was more a climb than a run. Dangerous, Grace might say, thinking not of a fall but of his heart. His legs were tying up badly, his legs were beside the point now, he was drawing on raw will and pride, the things that had kept him moving at a respectable pace in the dying laps of his 5,000 heat in Olympic Stadium thirty-four years ago, though he was punch-drunk and the other runners came gliding past him in a steady file, as if the lane next to him were a moving sidewalk. Their respirations—surreally distinct, stethoscopically loud—crashed in his ear. No other sound; the roar of the home crowd a sort of amplified silence. On the last lap his vision started to go, his brain hypoxic, blackness moving in from the margins. He collapsed on the finish line and lay heaving and for him as a serious competitor a finish line is what it was.

Just below the crest of the hill he veered back onto the trail and ran, or barely trotted, the last two hairpins. The cyclist would need another thirty seconds or more. Cutler topped the hill, gulping air as if surfacing after a full minute under water. Slowly his stride gained back its length, the jolting of the pulse in his jaw eased off. It was clear the cyclist must be heading back to the trailhead and parking lot, a mile farther on. No chance Cutler wouldn't lose badly if he and the man raced the whole way. Anyhow, he'd beaten him up the hill. Stop here, wave him past with a wry nod. *Nice try, dude.* Or slip away into the forest and run a shortcut—Cutler knew a good one—and so be there waiting for him at the trailhead, the finish line, grinning. Gratifying to think of that. Somehow Cutler couldn't bring himself to do it.

The gliding whirr of the mountain bike approached from behind him and he opened up his gait, fast but relaxed, fists loose, jaw floating. The trail here was level as it passed through another stand of maples and entered the tract of huge white pines he called the Basilica—not quite a cathedral-like grove of raincoast giants, but close enough, the trail running through a broad nave arcaded by stately, even-spaced trunks, while from ten storeys up, stained-glass light shafted downward, green and gold. A century's fall of pine duff had laid an ideal surface for running, silent, soft and fast. His favourite part of the trail. He and Mattie would start to recover their speed through here after the gruelling work of the

Reaper. And now he recalled that this was the place—
when Mattie was seventeen and Cutler was toughing
out an off day—that he'd first felt the boy carrying him,
holding back just a little for his father's sake.

He entered the grove at a controlled sprint, knowing
he could hold it to the far side, maybe four hundred
metres or so, and knowing that the cyclist would pass
him well before he reached that point. But he would
make him fight for it. Make him realize he had to work
to beat this guy on foot—this old man, as Cutler must
seem to him with his dated gear, his vulnerably thread-
bare scalp, a face creased and strained in the twilight
under the trees. Cutler's anger seemed gone now,
depleted or paid out, as at the end of the trial three
years back when he'd stood up and, before the bailiff
could intervene, addressed the man who had just been
convicted of reckless driving (a nine-month suspended
sentence). In his fixated way Cutler had rehearsed the
moment a hundred times, nights when the vodka and
Ativan hadn't bought him even a few hours' rest, and
he'd meant to holler one of several lashing denuncia-
tions he'd prepared. Instead he'd heard himself say, in
a voice that must barely have reached the convicted
man, "Are we just supposed to go home now?"

The only things that truly helped during those
months had been these forest trails and, above all,
Grace. Every night for months they lay twined without
ever having sex, a strange shift from all the years when
they had often made love but always slept a little apart.

The rider came sweeping alongside and past, his legs a blur, nostrils flaring as he exhaled in sharp little huffs. Cutler was almost grateful for this competitive serious-ness. He chose not to give the man a direct look, instead fixing his eyes on the trail, trying to retain his speed and stay relaxed and fluent, as dignified as possible for someone in late middle age who's red-faced, puffing, stumping along in a frantic race with a stranger. At some point a dead leaf had caught between the front mudguard and wheel of the man's bicycle and the shreds of it rattled in the blurring spokes like those hockey cards Cutler and his friends used to clothespin to the frames of their CCM three-speeds back in the early '60s, the cards smelling of the brittle wafers of bubble gum you would get in the twenty-five-cent packets. He could no longer recall why they'd wanted to set those cards—always some forgotten journeyman's card, never one of the stars—rattling in their spokes. Maybe there never was a reason.

The cyclist was pulling away uncatchably, Cutler fading, struggling to hold his form to the far side of the Basilica, and he thought again of Mattie, wondering if the boy and his friends had ever done the same thing with hockey or baseball cards when they were small. The brain, deprived of oxygen, always works poorly at this stage in a race; all the same, it bothered him that he couldn't remember.

[NEARING THE SEA, SUPERIOR]

The world being an ironist with poor taste and perfect timing, Neil Sedaka was on the oldies station crooning "Breaking Up Is Hard to Do."

"You know you don't have to do this," he said.

"You already said that, Erik."

"She was always crazy about you."

"You don't have to *say* that, Erik. I said I'd come. I just wish we could be honest with her."

His cellphone trembled in the breast pocket of his coat.

"Terminal 1, right?" the driver asked. He wore a topknot turban and had a wispy beard, no accent. He looked about sixteen. Rap or hip hop, you would guess, but he had the radio tuned to a pop oldies station.

"Terminal 1, yes."

The trembling in Erik's pocket stopped. In the over-heated car his brow and freshly shaven upper lip were damp, oddly chilled.

"Jason Singer actually got married in a hospital," he said.

"Jason."

"He had dinner with us last year. He and Ginny? First weekend in June."

"I don't know how you keep track of these things," she said.

"I like people, I guess."

She let that go. Then: "But 'first weekend in June'? I mean . . ."

"It was the second-last dinner we gave."

The cab started up an on-ramp leading into the airport. In his belly he felt the angle of their climb, a voluptuous sensation, cruelly out of context. The cab fishtailed on the sleety ramp and recovered. She checked her BlackBerry—it seemed their words had brought her own schedule to mind—then said, "The girlfriend was the flapper, right? Cloche hat, short curls?"

"Ginny. They were married. That's what I was saying. They got married in the hospital, in Jason's father's room. They moved the date up, so his father could be part of it."

Silence; she was back inside one of her designs. "What did her father have?"

"*Jason's* father. AIDS."

You don't listen. It was one of the first things that had

drawn him to her—a distractedness he'd mistaken for creative dreaminess, thus assigning soft edges to what was actually a tough, selfish trait: the quality that helped her gain a toehold in a field still vastly dominated by men. Porter—the name was her Virginian mother's maiden name—had a faculty of all-excluding focus that now struck him, at times, as inhuman. At other times he envied it. At all times it whetted his desire to possess her, which was now out of the question, and in fact, he realized, always had been.

"I don't recall much of that evening," she said shortly, as if irked at the expectation that she *should* recall it, though Erik had long since given up expecting such things.

"The conversation was scintillating," he said. "Especially yours."

She let her heavy, dark eyelids droop—her standard semaphore of warning.

"No, I mean it. You were. It amazes me you can't remember."

A few moments of silence, then she said, "It *is* too warm in here," and frowned, her thumb grazing his brow in an absent way, yet gently, as if she meant to taste the sweat there.

They had opposing views of social need. Neediness, in Porter's opinion, was the antithesis of charm; worse, those with needs could never be happy or free. To Erik, need was simply the adhesive that held the human world together. When especially frustrated he had thought of her, wrongly, he knew, as a sort of machine for transforming visual or verbal information into . . . well, all right, into truly original structures. Gorgeous structures. He was still her helpless fan.

In the terminal, on the moving sidewalk, they glided up the long concourse to the departure gates. It wasn't like her to stand behind him like this—or just to *stand*, instead of striding decisively onward. Petite, methodically put-together, she'd affixed her gaze to the bank of coffered skylights high above them, her estimation of the design unreadable. The supercilious arch of her brows, the satiric droop of her eyelids, the lines parenthesizing her mouth—all lent her a scornful look. Porter could look haughty patting a spaniel. He stared at her, rapt as always, knowing now that she was so absorbed in her study he was at low risk of receiving one of her fending glares.

Again his cellphone pulsed.

"They couldn't choose between a space pod or a greenhouse," she said.

I really should take this call, he thought.

An announcement rumbled out, slurred with echoes. It was too noisy, he told himself, to take the call.

"I think it's our flight," she said, glaring at her watch, then up at the ceiling. "There *has* to be a better way to control sound in these big volumes." She stalked past him in her long, lint-brushed coat, towing a carry-on bag in the brisk, territorial way of flight crew.

———

They had finally separated last fall. At times it amazed him that their misalliance had survived almost a decade. Still, there had been that certain bond. It was coded, he supposed, in his genes. His parents had spent their lives and raised Erik and his two older siblings up near Thunder Bay—dairy farmers in a subarctic zone, though to Erik's Finnish grandparents, who had lost their home to the advancing Soviets in '45, that had not seemed unduly daunting. Erik's mother had only really confided one thing about her and his father's marriage, and she probably hadn't meant to. At Paavo's wake, shaken but sturdy—drinking vodka and Coke, though not conspicuously drunk—she'd told the three children, "Thirty-two years we are married and never once he walks into the kitchen without that my stomach does like this." And her large, dry hand flipped over, exposing the pink, open palm. Some years later, when Erik related that anecdote to Porter, she'd said crisply, "You could interpret that sentence in two possible ways." Yet her gaze was evasive, as if the story unsettled her, imperilled her carefully managed self-containment.

"No, you couldn't," Erik told her. "Not if you ever saw them in the same room."

What wasn't said: that he and Porter had just the same connection. Whenever they were in each other's vicinity, a vital arc would leap the synapse between them, etching the air. Some friends even confided they could feel the charge. Porter loathed such talk. And in the sweaty aftermath of sex she would act as if nothing shocking had just occurred, as if she hadn't just been far beyond herself, cursing, laughing wildly, her hard little thighs crushing his hot ears and cheeks.

The flight had been called but wasn't boarding. Erik kept glancing out the wall of windows at their 737 and the runway—visibility poor—and at a display panel listing several departures as delayed. On a wide plasma screen bracketed down from the ceiling, the top-of-the-hour news: a panning shot of parked cars half-buried in snow. First delays, he thought, then cancellations. It was the time of year when this part of the earth is actually turning its face back toward the sun, yet winter goes on deepening its tenancy.

Further palpitations from his phone. Around the gate, passengers, seated, standing, had a herded, nervous look. Porter calmly sat and returned to her BlackBerry, emailing a response to a colleague's question (he guessed) or, possibly, sending a note to her new man. Her expression and posture gave no hint as to which of these she might be doing.

She and this new man were engaged, waiting for both divorces to come through.

In that state of applied absorption she brought to every task, she would not notice Erik taking the call. He walked past her, toward the food court, mumbling "Coffee?" No response. He took out the cellphone. It stilled in his hand. Three messages from Thunder Bay. He punched reply. Porter was juggling three projects these days and had made it clear, not unkindly, that if his mother died (she never used euphemisms like "passed away") before they could fly up there, she would not come along. Would not be able to. Though she might, if she could, still fly up for the day of the funeral.

The ringing was faint. Now another announcement. A pessimist would think *cancellation* but Erik was an optimist and he was finding that even divorce and grief left a basic stratum of one's character intact. The back of Porter's head—that practical pageboy cut of wondrous hair so straight and black—was still unmoving. She'd admitted, and she would never lie, especially not to be tactful or kind, that her fiancé was not the lover Erik had been. In fact he didn't seem to excite her at all. A senior partner in an architectural firm, he did command a better income than Erik, who was a high school guidance counsellor, but Erik believed the true issue here was that Porter desired to live *inside* her calling in every way, not just professionally but domestically, too. For some years, he saw, she had tried to slot their marriage into her life as a sort of moonlighting, or volunteer position, and she was incapable of sustaining a secondary passion. When she wanted to chat, it was about her work—her art—and "chat" was not the word.

"Rik, where have you *been?*" Anja's voice was panicked, chafed raw. "On the plane?"

"I'm here," he said quietly. "We're just leaving. How is she?"

"I can't hear! I've been calling and calling!"

"I'm sorry." He took a few more steps toward the food court. "How's—"

"What?"

"We're still in Toronto—we're about to board."

"We?"

"Porter's here."

"What? Porter's actually coming?"

"Yes," he whispered firmly.

Porter's demand for a divorce was a bitter blow, but Erik had been resigned to it and was even, yes, relieved, as if at last receiving a diagnosis he'd been expecting for years. Through much of the marriage he was unhappy— and yet, toward the end, it grew clearer to him that as someone of little worldly ambition he was just the sort of man cut out for happiness. It was Porter who had actually pointed this out to him—that the ambitious were never truly happy, that time terrified them, while for people like Erik time was no more than the benign, required solvent in which contentment could expand to the full. "You don't know how lucky you are," she'd told him, near the end. And while he could not yet feel it, he could sense, waiting beyond the grief he was just starting to surmount, a birthright of serenity and, in time, the large cheerful family he yearned for.

"Didn't think she'd come," Anja spat out, as if blaming Porter for something grave, their mother's condition being the obvious surrogate.

"Well, she keeps her word," he said, staring at the

back of Porter's head, his heart thudding, cellphone clamped to his temple. *The longer I keep Anja from saying what I think she has to say.* Each second, for one thing, kept his mother alive a bit longer.

"I'm so angry you didn't answer. I'm alone here now!"

"We . . . I'm sorry. I just couldn't. We're coming now."

"It's too late, Rik."

He opened his mouth to respond. Said nothing. Stared into the crowded food court. A beefy native man with a grey ponytail rushed two steaming paper cups toward a cashier. His grin was wide and wincing, as if he was enjoying the discomfort of the heat searing his hands.

Erik had told Porter he didn't want his dying mother to know about the divorce. Spare her that blow. Porter considered this dishonest but chose to make a concession. His mother, Maarit, had loved Porter, admired her. Maarit had been a talented pianist who, in the manner of women of her generation, had set aside her potential career and addressed herself to home and family. Perhaps rightly, she saw Porter's aloofness and unapologetic drive as the required traits of will that she herself might have deployed. Yet she betrayed no regrets about the conventional path she'd followed; perhaps it was truer to say that Porter's establishment in the family afforded a sort of proxy completion of her own cancelled journey. And Porter, as if understanding this—accepting, cherishing the role—had answered

Maarit's affection with unguarded warmth. Porter, flushed and serene of face, holding a wineglass of eggnog, her other bare arm atop the upright piano as Maarit on the bench played "O Holy Night": Maarit knew the second verse only in Finnish, not in the English she'd begun for her daughter-in-law's benefit, but now, seamlessly, Porter subbed in with the English words, singing with zest, if off-key. Erik gaped. It wasn't just that his wife was performing a song, a full *hymn*, which he had no idea she knew—she was also letting herself be seen and very much heard doing something inexpertly. She was more tenor than soprano and fell far shy of the soaring last note that Maarit herself, now singing in Finnish, easily hit, but both women seemed delighted, as if they had just performed a flawless duet on stage at Massey Hall. Erik was delighted too, clearing his eyes, clapping noisily, even as faint qualms of jealousy returned to him.

"Rikky?"

"When did it happen?"

"A few minutes ago."

"I thought we'd make it."

"Thank God you're coming! Jarmo and Gail are flying in from . . ." Anja's thin voice buckled. After some moments: "Vancouver. Tonight."

Erik lowered his face. His torso jerked as if he were taking punches under the heart. He had spent most of the Christmas break at his mother's side but had meant to be there at the end, too. And he saw that

he'd believed Maarit would hold on until he arrived—
the optimism of a youngest child who, as Porter once
remarked with undisguised envy, always knew himself
to be loved.

He glanced toward her now, expecting the beautiful
back of her head. Her face was on him, eyes deciphering.
She'd turned in her seat. People around her rising,
bustling. A line was forming. He reassembled himself.

"Rik?" Anja said.

"We're boarding, An. I'll see you in two hours."

"I love you," she said, and his heart seemed to
stagger.

"I love you too," he said. "I'm sorry."

He shoved the cellphone into his pocket and walked
straight toward Porter, who was studying him. He supposed she was hoping her journey would not be necessary. She had no time for it, of course. The wasted
airfare (he'd insisted on paying her way but she had
vetoed that) would be nothing to her. She spent more
on business dinners all the time. So he told himself. She
stood up, her face a collage of conflicting signals, and
embraced him in her new, sisterly manner, firm at the
shoulders but distinct at the waist. As their torsos met,
the smell of her, bitter cinnamon, clove, wafted in a
warm draft from under her charcoal cowl neck. Their
bodies would never divorce.

"I'm sorry, Erik."

He tightened his grip.

"I saw you crying there . . ."

He accepted her coming erasure from his life, but to have a few more days now—even a few more hours. If she stayed the night in his childhood home, they might make love again, a last time. There would be no stopping it. There never had been. Even now he felt the ambivalence in her embrace: her will's resistance, her body's deeper, disputing will.

He said, "It's just . . . Anja's in rough shape. You know how I am."

She pulled back, studied him with her interrogator's eyes: shale blue, deeply dubious. "You mean your mother's not . . . ?"

Say it, say it.

"We might still get there in time," he said.

She held his gaze—he didn't blink either—then winced a strange smile and looked at her bag: "Well, we better get on, then."

She led him into the line. To hide his face from her, his eyes flooding, he turned to the high plasma screen. Still the news. He couldn't hear the commentary but he recognized that dark shattered coastline: a view of Superior, the inland sea they would soon be flying over, taken from an aircraft moving out from shore. Completely iced over, it looked like a polar ocean. A few times a century these total freeze-ups occurred, though at the centre of the lake, it was said, a hundred miles out from land, an ice-free inner lake always remained, churning and steaming through winter's coldest nights.

[SWALLOW]

So, a job.

Your parents and many uncles and aunts would not call it a job. To them it would seem you've been institutionalized, which of course cannot be allowed to happen. Greek families do not allow such things to happen to their own. Greeks do not go into therapy or get hospitalized for schizophrenia or psychosis or anorexia nervosa and so on. Greek civilization, having lent those disorders their formidable names, cannot be expected to provide specimens as well. The bloodline is pure. And the community cares for its own—who, therefore, are less likely to need such intervention to begin with. Your father, the priest, often gives homilies on these very matters: inside your head. Inside this same crowded head your mother contributes antiphonally.

It's years since you've attended an actual service. Or a school. After high school you announced that you were taking a year off and moving in with your non-Greek boyfriend. A year off became several. In time, you moved out of Derek's place but you did not move home, chastened and remorseful, as expected. You've become one of those adults whose main contact with her parents is neural; you hear their hectoring voices in your head and, ever on the defensive, you reply (though these days you reply less often) and at times even trade sticho-mythic barbs with them in your dreams. As for Mega Sister and your younger brother and vast cast of cousins, until recently you saw them often enough and got along with them fine. And you have friends, Greek and non-Greek. Everyone agrees you are a cut-up, a rough treasure, a ready ear. Such a good ear.

Now a vast apathy has snowed you under. Not like an avalanche but a calm, soft, muffling midnight snow . . . on and on. It's not quite depression. You've been depressed twice before, in your teens. Mega Sister, engaged now, still living at home where she daily consults her secret, porn-like stash of self-help lit (why would a Greek household need such "help"?), explains your state as a "deferred reaction" to your breakup with DeRek Perish (that's how he spells Derek Parrish since leaving his folk-rock group to become lead singer for Thigh Master) two years ago. It's not. Greeks don't have *deferred* reactions, not even you, this inexplicably skinny, dreamy, addled young Greek. When Mega

Sister recites that you didn't grieve the relationship enough after it ended, you just nod at your cellphone. She knows nothing of your last month. It's never what people think it is anyway. The guy you've been seeing, Charles, tucks his sweaters into his jeans and every slot-lettered sign has a backwards N in it. Doesn't anyone else see how *exhausting* the world is?

Your new apathy, this inner deadness, isn't all bad. There's a sort of relief. A remission from all concern. Like the obliterating fatigue of a sleeping flu. Or heroin? Is this why people crawl into bed with hard opiates and stay there? Let the manic world go on chasing its tail—a yelping, spinning blur—you are in a ravine of stillness, silence.

Your parents and Mega Sister keep leaving messages: Uncle Lambros and Aunt Foula want you to waitress again at the Agora, even if you are too skinny and therefore a poor promotion for your uncle's excellent food. The messages don't mention your skinniness. Such references ended some while back, your parents and relatives increasingly concerned. Not that anorexia was ever your problem. You always ate all the food your aunt and uncle would ply you with, before your shift and after—the weight just wouldn't adhere. A bestiary of barbecued meats, roast potatoes drenched in olive oil, sautéed rice, *boureki*, *kataifi*, *galaktoboureko*, volcanic flaming cheeses . . . The problem was, you were an awful waitress. Forgetful, befuddled, clumsy. Unable to achieve that winning, waitressy charm, somewhere

between aloofly formal and invasively familiar. Oh—
and your Greek stunk.

You grope among uncertain objects under the bed for
the tiny cellphone, to call your uncle. Lifting it is like
hefting a curling rock—another thing you've lost interest
in doing. Twenty-six messages in all, four from Charles
of the tucked-in sweaters and three from Jayla, alleged
best friend. You stopped checking email ten days ago.

"*Theo* Lambros," you say thickly.

"Roddy!" he says in his cigar-smoked, mafia rasp.

"I'm sorry, I . . ."

"*Ochi, den pirazi, pethi!* You're going to come back to
us? I can give you a shift tonight, one of the girls is got
a cold."

"You know I'm no waitress."

"You're evolving! We work at it! The customers like
you, also."

"But you *fired* me."

"Just my temper," he says, and you picture him
shrugging, big grin, splaying his fat hands. He says,
"That man . . . he was city councillor and the *saganaki*,
it's like napalm. But come back. Your parents worry, you
have no idea. You sound so tired. You're not eating?"

"I'm starting another . . . I'm starting somewhere
else, tomorrow. That's the thing. But thank you. Could
you let them know I'm all right?"

"A new job? Where is this new job? You work in
another *restaurant?*"

"You know no other restaurant would give me a job."

"So, where?"

"It's . . . a clinic. A medical institution, of a kind."

"You're serving in their cafeteria!" he roars, not in the tone of someone who has cracked a mystery but of someone crushed by betrayal.

"I'm not," you say, and to pre-empt his next question you tell him, "I'm not working in the kitchen either." *There are businesses in the world besides the food service industry*, you want to add, but say nothing. This is just so exhausting.

"You're a nurse, then? But you haven't gone to school for nurse. Not a *janitor?*"

"Please don't worry. It's nothing like that."

"You haven't gone to school at *all* yet! Five years now!"

"And they'll pay me well."

"Of course! How else to get someone to work for a stranger?" His voice has the pitch of mystified contempt he uses when speaking of the doomed world beyond the frontiers of the Community. "Be careful! Don't get sick from all the sick people! Are you saving money to go back to school?" (The relatives keep expecting this of you, the best student the family has ever produced; your uncle still informs customers that you're "taking some time off.")

"Please tell Mom and Dad I'm fine. I might try to call them when the job is done."

You set the phone down and sprawl back amid your rancid sheets, spent to the last dram. You don't think you're ill, physically. It's more that things mattered and now they don't. You used to read ravenously. Now all curiosity has fled the premises. Your soul has dozed off for the duration. Is it shock, still? Guilt? Sounds like depression, but minus the ripping, visceral pain, the hurtling dread. Instead, a vacancy. Painless paralysis. Hard to believe your skull and ribcage are packed with pink and diligent organs, earnestly and ignorantly toiling, as in a coma victim.

All you want to do these days is sleep.

You might as well be getting paid for it.

The clinic is a hangar-like structure, cinderblocks and green corrugated siding, on the edge of an industrial park in the wind-scavenged steppes of outer Scarborough. At the park's entrance the bus drops you along with two women in matching peach parkas over grey sweats. A sunny sub-arctic afternoon. No sidewalks. Snowless lawns hard as Astroturf. Up the middle of the road the matched pals tow dark, wheeled suitcases as big as wolfhounds. You have only a daypack, yet they edge ahead, their trainers flashing, heads down, shoulders high and tight—the slapstick, puffin shuffle of Canadians in winter. You don't mind the wind's bee-sting assault on your skin. You haven't felt so awake in weeks. Neither do you mind the industrial park, finding something here that mirrors your inert inner world, so that for now—for a change—you don't feel out of place.

The doctor who draws your blood resembles some minor rock star of the '70s on a doomed comeback tour. Hair dyed brown, shaggy bangs, the rest hiding his ears, hanging to the collar of his lab coat. A haggard face, overexposed blue eyes. He's even thinner than you. There's a nameplate on the child-sized desk: DR. ARNOLD WALL.

He swabs your inner elbow.

"Try not to wince," he says in a tired growl. "I have to do this a lot."

There's a faint skunky smell that you can't quite place.

"Which trial are you?" he asks.

"Sedatives."

"You don't look like you need any."

"I just need the money," you say. "Sedatives pay better."

His atrophied face retracts and for a moment his eyes meet yours.

"That's why you all come here. I used to serve here when I was a med student. Not like me, now—like you. Test subject. And it wasn't just to put myself through med school, either. It was to be *involved* in the trial." He meets your gaze again, looks away, resumes as if against his will. "It was to make my own observations—I mean, besides being tested by the physician on site. There were a bunch of us like that, back then. We were all fascinated by the process. The *science* of it. Not like now. Times have changed. It's all about, about *money* now. I learned real important things serving here, I can tell you that, and we all, uh . . ."

Your silence and frank, receptive gaze always encourage people to blather, to over-represent themselves, till a moment of abashed realization. It's one of the traits that made you a regrettable waitress—diners would start unreeling their life stories and you couldn't very well walk away from the table while they yakked. Other diners, noticing, would complain. They wanted you to take their beverage order. They wanted to tell you *their* life stories.

"Anyway," he says gruffly.

"But it's for a drug company, isn't it? I mean . . ."

"It's still science. It's *important*."

You don't say "whatever," but you think it. You used to hate it when people said "whatever." Now you're a walking whatever.

"Your blood pressure," he says, seizing and shackling your arm in the Velcro sleeve.

"Oh . . . shouldn't that be *before* you take my blood?"

He gives you a face as he pumps the sleeve.

"Technically, sure. But why would you care about that? I mean, it's not like . . . not like any of you are *interested* in the findings—the process of it. No! But you all watch *ER* and reruns of, of *Marcus Welby* and you're eager to tell us all about *correct procedures*."

You wonder if this is where doctors come when all other options are exhausted.

"My God!" He stares at the gauge with marvelling eyes. "I've never seen anything like this. How are you feeling right now? Light-headed?"

"Not really."

"Systolic 84—diastolic 43!"

"I don't know much about blood pressure."

"This is *impossible*," he says, shaking his head. "It's not even legal!"

"What, there are laws?"

"Not legal for us to employ you, I mean. In the trial. Your BP is way below the normal range. My God!"

"Could I . . . do something to raise it a little?"

He stares at you intently, almost passionately. You stare back. The prospect of returning to your bachelorette, to the city, is unfaceable. Worse is the thought of defaulting on the rent. Having to move home. Your mother's and sister's gloating solicitude.

"I would like to stay, if possible."

"Sure—of course."

He leans into you. You lean away, wondering if he has misunderstood. His fixed, Rasputin gaze. In a voice almost secretive: "Here's what you do. Think of something, or some*one*, that upsets you very much. Fantasize about that person. Or thing. Now fantasize about . . . confronting them. About attacking them, even. Yes— even injuring them, quite badly. *Definitely* injuring them! Can you do that now?"

You wriggle a few inches down the crinkling, tissue-covered examination bed, away from Dr. Wall. You can certainly feel your pulse now, blood sluicing under your chin.

"See, your organism can't distinguish between an actual, external stress source and a merely *mental* stress source!" In his new enthusiasm he runs "stress" and "source" together so it comes out "stress horse." Like a euphemism for recurring nightmares.

"Is it working? Should we take another run at it?"

Lowering his head, Dr. Wall pumps with gusto. Grey roots, constellated dandruff.

"Okay! This one's more acceptable, if less interesting. Still a touch low, but legal. I'll enter this as your figure, okay? This technique always works. Seems everyone has somebody they can bring to mind to . . . to help them out. Bring the pressure up, or down."

"Thank you." You budge yourself forward and down off the bed, then make for the door. Your knees almost buckle, sloshing with the first adrenaline you've secreted in days. *Never look a stress horse in the mouth.*

"Just don't think of ever joining us for a BP medication trial!" he joshes, following you to the door with his clipboard, thoroughly cheered. "I mean, unless you go and *marry* the guy. Go choose your bunk now. Or grab a coffee. Cafeteria's at the end of this hall and to the left. As long as this blood clears, the trial starts at five. See you again tomorrow morning! Oh, and I'm sure I don't need to mention . . . ?"

By the time you enter the windowless dorm, seven of the eight beds are occupied, by bodies or luggage. Four double-decker bunks that might be summer

camp cast-offs or army surplus. Low lockers between
them. Walls the colour of overcooked greens, two
banks of fluorescent tubes on the ceiling: the sickly
atmosphere of a cheap chop suey house at two a.m.
You drop your daypack on the lower bunk—someone
is already asleep, turned to the wall, on the upper
one—and creak down on the mattress beside a little
pile of folded, bleach-bright sheets, a couple of thin
grey blankets, a foam pillow.

The pair of friends you saw earlier have already
made up the bunk beds across from you. It's as if they've
been installed for weeks. On the top berth, the one
with the platinum dye job is on her back with MP3
earbuds in place, hands behind her head, eyes closed,
toes tapping the rung at the foot of the bunk. Eggplant
toenail polish. She has changed into pyjamas and is
chomping gum in time to her tunes, some kind of rap/
hip hop mix. The other—still in her sweatpants and a
salmon tank top, gelled spiky hair with brunette
streaks—is in the lower bunk, belly down, propped on
her elbows reading a book. In the shadows above her
shoulder, a couple of four-by-six photos tacked to the
wall: a solemn young man, a grinning husky.

These women must be regulars. They have that
blasé, territorial assurance, and normally, as a novice
outsider, never the alpha of any group, you'd feel
uneasiness—the need for deference so as to earn
your way in—but now, well. Whatever. You sag onto
the bunk, look up at the mesh of rust-pocked struts

supporting the hammocked mattress above you. Your eyes close.

"Going to sleep already, are you?"

It's the bottom one, you think, addressing her friend, but then in a more intentional tone, with some kind of English accent, she throws out, "You should save it till later."

You roll onto your side, politely facing her, though without sitting up.

"First time, is it? It's always easy to tell. What's your name?"

"Roddy."

"There's a first." She flips her fat book closed and twists her upper body toward you, as if to show off her plumped-up cleavage. "I'm Hannah."

"It's short for Ariadne." (Your parents called you Philomela, but you've come to insist on your middle name, short form.)

"Another first," says Hannah. "You should call me Han. And this is Wendy. Wen." She nods upward and Wen turns her head toward you, opens her huge blue eyes and nods, then turns away again, stridently chewing.

"What do you think of Keith Richards, then?" Han asks, then saves you the breath by saying, "The doc. Dr. Wall. Always trying to 'check my heartbeat.'" She inserts the punctuation with fingertips and arched brows. "Trying to get his stethoscope in here."

"But he's a *doctor*, dear," a voice says soothingly from

the back of the dorm. "He's only doing his job." In the shadows of a lower bunk sits a middle-aged woman who seems to have sprung from a TV series of decades ago—housedress, matronly spectacles, high-piled turban of liver-coloured hair. She's cross-legged on the bed and the posture seems paradoxical. The peak of her hair touching the upper bunk. A Harry Potter novel closed in her lap.

"And what's wrong with my pulse *here?*" Han asks, raising a fisted forearm, as if in some Girl Power salute.

"Well, all I know is he did the same to me, dear."

"Anyway," Han says, turning back toward you, "I reckon he won't bother you. How do you stay so thin anyway? I think you look fabulous."

"You look nice, too," you say slowly, waves of slumber foaming toward you—up, up the pebbled beach they come with a snoring rattle. You used to have awful insomnia. That seems a foreign life now, another physique. What could be easier than yielding to this mild, voluptuous tide?

"If I could lose maybe eight pounds," Han says.

"Guess it's hard to exercise at a place like this," you say, as if the prospect concerns you.

"Out of the question entirely is more like it. They won't install a workout room because it would cost them. They say you can walk the halls, or walk outdoors between blood tests, but who's going out *there* and where would you fucking walk to anyway?"

"We will be sharing this room for three days," the older woman says peaceably, eyes on her opened book.

" . . . over to FedEx? So we just lay about. There's a TV room. This time'll be worse, too. We'll all just be sleeping—I reckon."

"You mean you haven't done sedatives before?"

"Always avoided them," Han says. "But they raised the pay for them because somebody had, like, a bad reaction last year. That's what we hear. So now we want to try sedatives, because of the pay."

"Someone died?"

"Nobody'll give the story. There isn't even much on the net, just rumours, on blogs and places like that. These people are good. This is quite the little industry."

Her accent seems to be set on Intermittent. The older woman, now sitting on the side of her bed, works her feet into a pair of fierce-faced schnauzers with plausible eyes. Support stockings the creepy colour of mannequin skin hug her fat calves. She stands slowly, a hand braced on her lower back. A little, stoic smile.

"I won't be a moment, girls."

"Bye," you say. She shuffles across the olive lino-leum, picks up speed in her lapdog slippers, pushes through the swing door.

"She looks too old," Han says. "Like, over the limit. And you—you look like you could be under. But no worries." She glances significantly toward the door and lowers her voice: "We're all getting round the system one way or another, aren't we? You're meant to take a month off before checking in again, but there are these other clinics. Three in Toronto, one in Guelph, one in Kingston. If you bounce around between them you can be doing it all the time. Sometimes your first blood test won't clear because there's, like, residual contaminants from the last trial? Then you have to wait a bit, but mostly it's fine. They don't ask a ton of questions. I'm putting myself through school like this. Never made so much money in my life."

The door swings and a clump of women enter, briskly herded by a nurse, the physical antimatter of Dr. Wall: black, tall, buxom, bristling with vitality. Or is it anger? Her plucked eyebrows converge on a stern crease between her eyes.

"A few words before we begin. To your bunks, please," she says in a voice that seems layered like phyllo pastry—a schooled British accent superimposed over others that bubble to the surface on certain words. It's a trait you know from your relatives. Accents are an acoustical fossil record of an immigrant's journey. She carries a tray with small paper cups, a plastic pillbox.

The women spread out to their bunks. The first looks Chinese, around forty, in sunglasses and Bermuda shorts and knee socks and penny loafers. Her tucked-in man's shirt is the colour of the walls, as if, despite her outfit, she's hoping to blend in. She scales the rungs at the end of the bunk she'll be sharing with the older woman, now shuffling back into the dorm. In the next top bunk there's a small, exhausted-looking South Asian girl—skin grey, not brown—above a burly woman with a raw, blunt, ruddy face. Camouflage headscarf over cropped white hair, loose denim jacket and pants, work socks, German sandals.

"Good afternoon. I am Nurse Nkwele. We will now commence trial C134. In a moment, you will be taking a full regular dose. Afterwards, you may proceed to the cafeteria. Or to the lavatory, just outside in the corridor, to your right. Or for a short walk. But you had best be back and upon your bunks within twenty minutes." Parade square pronunciation, an abolishing gaze she sweeps across all faces. "Thirty at the most. You should become drowsy and lose consciousness within an hour. Unless you fight it. I don't recommend that you fight it. Nor that you drink much tea or water before your subsequent doses. You can expect to sleep for at least six hours. That is, until eleven p.m. Certain of you will continue to sleep after that. However, you will be awakened at midnight to receive a second dose and to submit to a blood draw. We will be drawing your blood at four-hour intervals. Mobile telephones to be disengaged between the hours of eleven and the time of your third dose, eight a.m. I will brook no exceptions. Are there any queries?"

Nurse Nkwele stands before each subject to dispense a pill. She does not move on until the pill has been swallowed. For some time she ponders the greyish girl on her upper bunk, who is throwing her head back like a dummy in a safety film where they repeatedly show a rear-end crash.

"Relax yourself," Nkwele commands. "Relax the throat." The girl's eyes bulge with panic. At last her tiny Adam's apple buoys and she exhales and chugs the water in the paper cup crimped in her hand.

"It's bitter," she says in a grade-school voice. "I'm sorry. I've a hard time swallowing."

"How old are you, girl?"

"I'm eighteen."

"Too young!"

"But . . . they said eighteen was the legal age."

"Which is why you said eighteen. As opposed to, say, seventeen. Or fourteen."

"Miss, eighteen is the age that I am!"

Her voice will break. Nurse Nkwele actually emits a *Hmmph!* and moves on. As she approaches, you know you should get up, or at least sit up, but inertia, like the pressure of stacked atmospheres, has pinned you. She has to stoop down with the tray.

"Now—what is languishing you so?"

Her hands are strong and long-fingered. The wedding ring, a fleck of diamond on a slim gold band, seems incongruous, a child's pretend ring, too small and the sort of thing a nurse removes before a shift to avoid damage.

"You have a touch of flu," she says. "At the least. You should not be here either."

"I'm fine," you say. "Honest." And you reach for the drug, that enticing, tiny pillow, blue as the walls of a nursery.

"Expecting honesty here is like expecting song and dance in a fracture ward," she says in a wide, inclusive voice. "I know which among you are going from clinic to clinic and I would put a stop to it if I were in charge."

From across the room, Han and Wen roll their eyes at Nurse Nkwele's broad back. She's packed into her white coat like a superhero in a stretchy suit. You swallow. You too find the act difficult at times. At the root of your tongue, the bitter taste registers just late enough that you don't gag.

"What are these pills called?" you ask, to switch the topic and because you adore the names of pharmaceuticals—and sedatives are best, little lullabies of syllables.

"The T81-B. It isn't named as yet. It isn't approved as yet. It depends on these trials and so forth."

Dormazone, you invent silently. *Serenalude.*

"Normally you would come to get the pills yourself," she says, straightening. "Normally I don't serve the test subjects. It is different with this trial, of course. You should not be walking around too much. You understand?"

You understand the part she means you to understand: not that you shouldn't be walking around too much, but that she doesn't normally serve people this way.

She looks upward, presumably at the stranger in the top bunk, and says dryly, "Wake up now—time for your sleeping pill."

Lunaquil. Celestanox.

The bed struts rearrange themselves with grudging reluctance, scraping, squeaking.

"Ah," says Nurse Nkwele, "and who have we here?"

You walk down the long hallway and there's a window! To the southwest, a flat horizon ruptured by a few distant clumps of apartment blocks: surviving monoliths of a nuked city. How will you live there anymore? A blood-clot sun sinks into clouds of surgical gauze.

The cafeteria is not a separate room but a service counter cut into the wall and, in front of it, a roped-off area that fills and blocks the hallway. There are some white plastic tables and chairs where a few people sit alone—two women, one man. By the entry/exit on the far side, an easelled sign reads MALES ONLY PLEASE THIS SIDE OF CAFETERIA. You enter from the women's side, passing a blank sign and glancing back: WOMEN ONLY ON THIS SIDE, PLEASE! You're in a small demilitarized zone of gender overlap. Curious dates must occur here, guys full of tranquillizers or erectile dysfunction drugs trying to flirt, groggily or urgently, with gals on hormone replacements or prescription laxatives; just as in real life.

Only the face of the attendant shows above the counter, which is not especially high. She has a sepia headscarf, the dark and sun-dried face of an Inca mummy. You'll have the ham and tomato on brown. Scowling, she counts out your change in a rhythmic, alien mutter, as if casting a curse. You slump at a table near the payphone. The bread is waterlogged. The tomato tastes sinister—bitter green. Drug T81-B? A life, you guess, can become mere aftertaste. You shuck the black clamshell of your cellphone and tap a button: as expected, another message from Charles and another from Jayla. You're about to snap it closed when you see a call coming in silently.

It amuses you, slightly, to think of dozing off mid-conversation.

"Jayla Harviss," you say.

"Roddy! Finally! Where are you?"

"Scarborough."

"God, what are you doing out *there?* Fuck, I've been so worried! And Charles, he's been worried sick about where you are. We're *all* worried about you. Charles actually went to your place yesterday and let himself in—well, both of us, actually."

"Sorry about the mess."

"Mess . . . ? God, just . . . are you all right, then?"

"You didn't like Charles at first," you tell her.

"What?"

"Worrying about me has brought you closer together."

A pause, then: "Like I said, Rod—we're all worried. We don't know why you just, like, disappeared."

"You must have a mutual theory by now."

"Roddy, you . . . what? But . . . you know how *there* we are for you, Rod! Roddy . . . ?" Her voice, brash and laughing, has a throttled thinness now. You imagine the pupils in her lovely lavender eyes: constricted, all but gone. "Roddy . . . you sound really weird. Are you—"

"Fine, but the sedatives should take effect any moment, so I better go."

"Sedatives. Oh my God! Should I be, like, calling someone? Roddy!"

"It's . . . let me see. *Serenalude*. I just took one."

"You . . . bitch!" She sounds like Jayla now. "Don't fuck around with me this way!"

"But I don't," you say, the bitter taste refluxing in your throat and mouth. "I don't fuck around with friends. Or with friends' friends." And you clip the phone closed on her tiny chatter, the voice of a genie who no longer holds sway over you.

The older woman, her beehive dismantled, now wearing a hairnet, pulls the covers to her chin, then sets her open Harry Potter face-down on her chest. She says brightly, "Let's introduce ourselves. We'll go in a circle, clockwise. I am happy to begin."

Wen, prone on the bunk, and Han, standing beside it in a bra and thong, pulling on her pyjamas, roll their eyes again, though it seems perfunctory, lacking malice.

"I am Eleanor Morris. I am from Thunder Bay, but I just moved to Toronto to take care of my old father. He's over ninety now. My sister helps some. I do these sessions every now and again to make a little money for us—and to take a break from Dad!"

She removes her glasses with both hands and, turning carefully in bed, places them in the schnauzer slippers aligned on the floor next to her. An arm of the glasses goes in either slipper, each wide lens a windscreen over the eyes of either dog.

The Asian woman above her says, "Me, I am Hong. Come to Canada last summer. From China. Chengdu. But no work here. The, the *relatives*"—for a moment she fights the word, then pins it impressively—"give no help here. *Mayo*. Because I am Christian now, I think. That's all."

Both women in the next bunk are silent for a second, politely waiting each other out. Then the bearish woman in the lower bunk says, "I go by Ruth. I'm a paralegal. Work with homeless folks, mainly women." Her clipped voice has a tightly managed tone. A big, confident voice undercut by something. Is that how the drug is hitting her?

"I imagine you must be here," Eleanor says, "because they keep taking away the funding for work like yours?"

"It's not really that."

"Well, it's a crime, in my opinion."

Silence. When the South Asian girl on the upper bunk realizes Ruth the paralegal is finished, she says, "Oh, I'm Sunetra. Just trying to save money to go to school in the fall! At Ryerson. Are *you* in school?" She looks straight at you, then across at Han and Wen. In unison Wen says, "No," and Han says, "Part-time— biology, York."

They look at you expectantly. You're still on your feet, though wobbly, fumbling to tuck the sheets over the rubber mattress cover, a stoned nurse trying to change a comatose patient.

"It's Roddy. I'm taking a little time off school."

"That is the *coolest* name," says Wen. "Do your friends call you Rod?"

"You can if you like."

"Right fucking on. Hot rod. Hot name."

"And what about you?" Han says, looking at the motionless shape above you.

"I think she may already be fast asleep," says Eleanor, squinting blindly. "Has anyone talked to her yet?"

No answer.

"Roddy is short for Ariadne," Han tells Wen.

"Doesn't that mean, like, spider or something? In Arabic?"

The door blows open: Nurse Nkwele with her clipboard held to her bosom.

"It is now a quarter to six. Unless anyone objects, I will close the main light."

Beside the door, a *Henry's Moon* nightlight glows in a socket. An odd, homey touch. A nursery touch. You've given up on making the bed. The mattress is quicksand.

Your own soft gasp wakes you. A Cyclops with an eye of blue laser light looms above, prodding at you. Now you feel the needle—not entering your arm but already there.

"It's just a blood draw, girl. You go back to sleep."

"You're done?"

"Likely you'll not even remember."

Your eyes close. Must be four a.m. Nurse Nkwele moves on, her passage tracked by the faint shunt of a cart's wheels, her rubber soles professionally silent. Murmuring now to someone else. The door swings, a triangle of sallow light fans open, closed. Surgical tape pinching the down of your forearm. You never felt her apply it. Nothing for a while, a dreamless gulf, then Charles, in the form of a fog named Marcus Welby, seeps into your twilight. The fog doesn't look like Charles but of course you recognize him. He's explaining why he sometimes tucks his sweaters into his belted jeans and khakis. It accentuates the V-shape of the male torso! His bleached hands carve a strident V in the air. You're semi-conscious now. Late Sunday breakfast in a diner booth. You're not a smoker but you miss the smell of cigarettes now that smoking is banned in restaurants—it was part of the experience of the hungover, sex-sore, greasy spoon brunch.

"But it looks strange," you say.

Charles strokes his stubble. *See*, he means, *I have stubble! I look incredibly manly with stubble!* Bestowing a patient smile, he says, "To a woman's eye; better a good body in unstylish clothes than a shapeless body dressed in style."

"That's the women's eye-view, is it?"

"Untucked is shapeless," he sums up. "*QED.*"

"You've canvassed a lot of female opinion?"

He blinks behind his eyewear. "One picks this stuff up. I overhear conversations, I see a sentence in a magazine, or something in a book by a woman. I triangulate."

"Anyway, Charles, you don't *have* a V-shaped torso"—as soon as you say this, you repent of your cruel candour—"and you look good the way you are. You're good untucked!"

"But it's about the success of the illusion!" he cries. "That's what matters these days!" He's doing an MA in philosophy and wants to be a "public intellectual," the sort who appears on TV semi-shaven and says relevant things in a cool way. In other words, a rock star. (Too bad about his clothes sense.) He talks on vehemently, desperate to win his point. His hands are small and soft, but in motion they're dynamic.

A cellphone bip-bips light years away. Have you not turned off your cellphone? But it's been off for weeks. *So why did you even bring it?* A therapist might see your decision as a positive sign, leaving one valve of contact unclosed. To you now it seems a symptom of weakness.

Someone answers in a whisper. Right above you. A low whisper—low as in soft and low as in baritone. Low for a woman.

"So-so. But I can't talk now. I'll tell you tomorrow how it's going."

That fanning flash of light again, Nurse Nkwele thrusting in like a Valkyrie.

"Turn it off or I will take it from you."

"But—"

"Or I will take it from you."

Further currents vessel you warmly and you imagine they will soon perfect a sedative that banishes all dreams, even memories.

Dr. Wall, haggard but happy, is reading your blood pressure in his office. It smells like he smokes in here. It smells like he *sleeps* in here. It's eight a.m. and an ancient day nurse has ushered seven of you (the inmate in the bunk above you has been hard to rouse) into the doctor's drunk tank of a waiting room, then re-drugged you. A troupe of ghouls: Sunetra asleep on Eleanor's shoulder, Han and Wen leaning into each other, head to head, lips open, eyes shut. Hong nodding over a laptop. Ruth's big arms buckled hard across her torso as if to suppress her trembling; eyes scrunched closed, brow damp.

Dr. Wall calls you in first. "And how was my star patient's first night?"

"Okay, thanks. That pinches."

"Especially with a small arm like yours!" He pumps with vigour, his tongue touching his upper lip. "This should be interesting. Hope you don't mind if I, uh, make some clinical notes on you."

"Is Ruth okay? That large woman, the paralegal. She's got the shakes."

Absently, eyes fixed on the gauge, he says, "Not to

worry, Ms. Kanakis. I'm watching her and that's all just tickety-boo."

"I hear something happened with an earlier sedition trial . . ."

He blinks, then shows his pleasure. His incisors are white, canines yellow.

"I mean *sedative* trial!" you say.

"See, that's one of the symptoms! This is good—this is what we were expecting!" If his hands were free, he'd be rubbing them together. "By essentially *paralyzing* the verbal/logical part of the brain, this drug makes it possible for neurotics and worriers and so on to achieve a state of restful sleep. But! There's a bit of a hangover, especially after a double dose, and sometimes the wrong words come out. Fascinating, huh?"

A faint pneumatic sigh as the sleeve releases.

"Yup, you're still reading low. I'm wondering if this might be an unusual rebound effect of the presumed pregnancy."

You stare at him.

"Your blood tests suggest you were recently pregnant. The low BP coinciding with it might be a complete 'coincidence,' sure, but I find the correlation pretty suggestive. You *were* recently pregnant?"

"I miscarried. It was early on."

"And *did* you have a history of low blood pressure before?"

Suddenly you're too depleted to respond. You look down, bite your lower lip to steady it. Too late.

After some moments Dr. Wall, now stiffly sheepish, says, "Sorry about the miscarriage."

"Okay."

"They're real common, more common than people think," he adds, and he proffers what he has—data and stats—as consolation: "Up to 45 percent, in fact, according to one school of thought. And some feel the incidence is rising, possibly as an effect of, and this is fascinating, a general weakening of the gene pool due to the way the usage of antibiotics has, uh, prevented the natural triage among weak and strong offspring over the last forty or fifty . . ."

It was a shock, the pregnancy. A real stress horse. Within days it altered you, like a potion or a serious illness. For one thing, it made you fall in love with Charles, who until then you'd been unsure of. (You see now that you were also tickled at the thought of presenting your parents with a tiny blond Anglo bastard.) After five days, sure of your feelings, you gave Charles the news. Nervously you feigned neutrality, so as to draw a candid response, but he must have sensed your excitement. "That's *amazing!*" he exclaimed, though with the look of a man congratulating a rival on winning a huge fellowship. He pounced, embraced you, hid his face behind your ear.

"What's wrong?"

"NOTHING!" he said, rending your eardrum. "But . . . are you sure we want to do this?"

"Others," Dr. Wall says, "blame environmental

toxins, especially those with long half-lives in the body."

"But I don't understand, Charles. A few days ago you were talking *marriage*."

"But I know it's hard. My ex-wife miscarried when we were not much older than you. We came here from the States after college, in '68. The war. I went to med school here. Really I wanted to be a researcher."

"A father is just not how I feel right now, Rod."

You're touched that Dr. Wall is making an effort this way. He is so wooden, it's obvious he hasn't had much practice. Or is he just afraid of losing his star patient?

You go on thinking about Charles while Dr. Wall does a second reading.

"Well," he announces, "it worked again!"

Day two passes like a day in a tropical fever ward. Even when the first cycle of pills wears off, around three p.m., everyone is flattened. The women doze, go out to the washroom or for a short walk—nobody feels like walking for long—or to purchase a pretty much futile coffee. Sunetra wandered off to the TV/computer room after the last blood draw and has not been seen since. The baritone in the bed above you is still asleep, turned to the wall, the collar of a grey fleece tracksuit visible where the blanket ends. A beige near-afro of curls like wood shavings. Huge black sneakers on the locker. Eleanor, still in her hairnet, is propped on her bed with Harry Potter on the lectern of her knees. Every fifteen minutes or so she turns a page. On the upper bunk, Hong slumps against the wall with her laptop open on her thighs, greasy hair tied back, lips moving while she reads. She improves her English by studying Scripture, she says; she has the full text of the King James Bible on her hard drive. Han, prone on her mattress, is browsing *Cosmo*. Maybe she's given up on trying to study while here.

"Listen to this—champagne contains traces of lithium. So it's a natural mood-booster."

Wen takes out an earbud and says, "Could losing all this blood hurt us? I mean, in combo with the drugs?"

"That's what they're trying to find out, dear," Eleanor says without looking up. "If the drugs are dangerous."

"What means 'graven'?" Hong asks Eleanor, who's helping with her English.

"It means 'carved,' I believe—isn't that correct?" Eleanor squints over at you.

"What's the sentence?" you ask.

"They're really not taking much blood," Han says. "Oh, and it's a myth about the bubbles making you drunk faster."

"*Behold, I have graven thee upon the palms of my hands.* Isaiah 49:16."

"I guess it would mean more like 'cut,'" you say. "Like with a razor or piece of glass."

Hong nods firmly, as if mechanically locking the definition in place. Eleanor beams at you and says, "I can always tell the bright ones. I ought to have taught school!"

You know this is a cue of some kind but you're too weary to respond.

"Wouldn't mind a drink about now," Wen says. "Not champagne. A shooter and a pint. And a *smoke*. That's the only time I still want one."

Ruth, on her back with her eyes closed, rolls dramatically toward the wall as if brusquely ending an argument with an invisible bedmate.

"God!" says Wen. "Aren't we even allowed to talk during the *day?*"

"I have commandments!" Hong says, holding up a piece of paper that must be the contract you didn't bother reading. "It says, to talk in the dorm in the day not forbidden."

Charles is back. Charles who donates blood and always makes a show of not needing a rest afterward. He has a nice-looking face and a slim, waifish body—a combination highly appealing to girls who wear layered black and listen to Nick Drake and Leonard Cohen— but he hates his body and weight-lifts with punitive diligence. He's one of those twenty-three-year-old guys who always seems to be shimmering with rage, and the rage comes because the world will not ratify and reward his brilliance. That he has yet to provide the world with firm evidence doesn't occur to him. The world should just sniff it out on him. And where does it come from, you wonder, this deep, aggrieved conviction of one's genius? What a luxury! Even in your last year of high school, when teachers were all telling you *you* were brilliant, a talented writer with a great career ahead, university, grad school, anything you chose, you found it hard to have faith in yourself. Yet in every class there was a student—usually a boy, though not always—who, while getting far less encouragement than you, still stubbornly believed in his own radiant destiny.

After you gave blood together at a clinic, Charles said, "Hey, they say I have A+ blood!" He cocked an ironic eyebrow, yet you sensed he was secretly chuffed. All the same, you felt for him—more and more as you grew intimate with his better features, his idealism, his earnest curiosity. You knew he suffered. In a world where there isn't enough importance to go around, men like him, who need a lot of it, will always be disappointed.

Another psychotropic doze and you decide to get some food, though your appetite is dead, stomach vacant but gassy, as Nurse Nkwele warned might happen. She'll be back on shift before long, bearing the next dose. You slump up the hallway, stand at the window. The only sign of life in the industrial park is a bird—some kind of swift or swallow?—that keeps plunging straight out of the sky toward the mouth of the chimney of the building next door. At the last moment, over and over, this small diver peels away as if losing faith, then loops up again to try a fresh approach. Finally it triumphs—keeps its sickle wings tucked flat and zips straight down the shaft—and though you've been rooting for the bird until now, its final success disturbs you. As if its vanishing was not voluntary; as if it has been sucked into the engine of a private jet.

Another marshy sandwich, salmon salad. It tastes wrong, the coating in your mouth scrambling the flavours. The only other diner is a short, bearded guy in a tank top, doubled over a table, pushing away his paper plate of food—laminated *moussaka*, oily fries and a "Greek salad" of iceberg lettuce with feta flakes. Now he grips his paunch and makes faint, crooning moans. You're unsure if you're meant to hear. Maybe he wants you to ask if he's okay. Normally you would. You avert your gaze and a pair of dark eyes, banefully watching you from the pass-through counter, look away. The curse of the Inca mummy. You're feeling a little paranoid. A symptom you should probably report at the next blood draw. Then again, ha ha, what if they should use it against you.

The washroom: your face in the mirror, in unchivalrous overhead light, lips rabid with toothpaste. You're scrubbing hard, teeth and tongue and way back in your mouth, almost gagging yourself as you scrape away that caustic aftertaste. You look even thinner. Jayla has always told you she envies you your Mediterranean cheekbones. Women with cheekbones, she says, never age.

"Do you think I look *green?*" Wen asks loudly, her huge blow-dryer in hand. She's grooming at the next sink, a towel wrapped around her from just above the nipples to just below the crotch. She's exhaustively waxed. She has swabbed off her metallic blue eye-shadow but still wears pink lipstick.

"I think it's just the lighting," you say.

"And I'm breaking out around the mouth. Han said it can be a symptom of like, poisoning? Like if someone spikes your drink in a club, you break out around the mouth the next day?"

"Wouldn't that be the least of your worries the next day?"

"Hmm, right." She nods vaguely. "Plus, I'm packing it on. All this lying around. Food's better than I expected. You don't seem to be having any problem."

"Actually, I think you look great," you tell her, hoping that'll be the end of it, but in the mirror you see her face snap toward you, a sunrise of colour coming to her cheeks and throat as she smiles. A lovely smile. And you're glad you said it. Her fingers bracelet your wrist, squeezing. She doesn't realize the industrial blow-dryer in her other hand is now trained on you, point-blank. In the mirror you see your hair shooting back and your eyes squinting, as if you're riding a Harley, free and easy, a hot Nevada wind in your face.

"You're sweet," Wen says megaphonically. "But you're so quiet! Are you okay? You want to use my Conair on your hair? I mean, after you wash it a bit?"

"Thanks."

The blow-dryer goes on sandblasting your face, searing the tear ducts. You're strangely moved—a combination of Wen's unexpected humanity and that mirror flash of yourself as everything you no longer are.

Returning to the washroom just after five, after taking the first pill of the next cycle, you chuck your cellphone in the garbage bin and rearrange things over it. You've stopped checking to see if messages are amassing. A sound from the far stall and you recognize the large shoes, black Converse sneakers, that have sat on top of the locker for the last twenty-four hours. They're facing the toilet. As you stare, something occurs to you. You flee and hurry back to the dorm. You lie on your bunk, hearing the other women talk and begin to slow, slur, go silent, as you wait for your bunkmate to return.

Ruth is mopping her face with a white T-shirt.

"Are you all right, Ruth?" asks Eleanor.

"Holding my own. Thanks."

"Touch of flu?"

"I'm good," she says, then adds conclusively: "Thanks."

Hong asks Eleanor, "What this whole verse means? *For thy waste and thy desolate places . . . shall even now be too narrow by reason of the inhabitants, and they that swallowed thee up shall be far away.*"

"I think it has something to do with overcrowding, don't you think, Roddy?"

Wen gives you a collegial leer. She's changing into a T-shirt that says TO SAVE TIME, LET'S JUST ASSUME I KNOW EVERYTHING. Sunetra is snoring—soft, demure little snores.

You nod, still waiting; but you drift off before the eighth dorm-mate returns.

It's the middle of the night and you're packed with narcotics and suffering your first insomnia in weeks. When guardian vampire Nkwele slipped in an hour ago to wake you for the blood draw, you were globe-eyed in the darkness, staring at the bunk above you. Rebound insomnia, she explained—it occurs with almost all sedatives, although the manufacturers were hoping that it would not with this one. That way (she said in a whisper thick with distaste) patients would not have to take occasional hiatuses from them. They could sedate themselves nightly. Forever. And some physicians would happily facilitate such a course. She would not, however, if she were practising.

"Plus, I feel uneasy," you told her, not wanting her to go. Wishing she would sit maternally on the side of the bunk, though half ashamed to explain your fear.

She said she would note down that symptom as well. *Uneasy.*

Now the big stranger above you is tossing. To your relief, Han and Wen are also awake, Han whispering softly, Wen loudly. Her hearing has been damaged; not everyone can be a rock star but now everyone can have rock-star hearing. She keeps saying "*What?*" so that Han has to raise her own volume.

"The realm of possibility's a pretty big place, Wen."

"So, you really don't like doing that to Rick?"

"I'm okay with it. But I don't really like when he does it to me."

"Oh my God, are you serious? Is he, like, no good at it?"

"I get lonely. He seems so far away. You know?"

"I certainly do not!" Wen shrieks. "I feel like I'm being *worshipped*."

After a silence Han says, "So maybe being worshipped is a lonely thing."

"Not being worshipped is lonelier any day."

Is the bunk above you moving steadily, vibrating?

"Be quiet, please!" Hong hisses. "There is a time to rest, and we're on drugs."

"So *go* to sleep," Wen says. "We're not stopping you."

"Wen," Han chides—and it hits you that her accent has all but vanished.

You roll toward the wall. Didn't Sylvia Plath say, "How I would like to believe in tenderness"? Easier to believe from a safe remove. Think of your sweet uncle, for instance. Or Mega Sister. Don't think of Charles. *Don't, Charles*. Sharing a bed is no safe remove. *Please, don't*. When he was about to come that way, he would hold your head down and in your last weeks together he had clamped it down as far as it would go, like a movie villain drowning somebody in a river. And you were drowning, you were choking. No more, you finally said. You called Jayla to talk about Charles and your various concerns and to tell her that you were pregnant and weren't sure what to do, given his obvious reluctance and his increasing roughness, but you didn't get as far as the pregnancy. Because when you said, "I don't even mind doing it like that—usually I *like* it," she cut in, "You don't *mind?* I love it!" She even loved having her head forced down in a death grip, she said. The thrilling insistence of it. The *vehemence*. And that word, "vehemence," was simply not native to Jayla's vocabulary. Not her style at all. "Vehemence" was Charles's style.

A numb, plunging sensation in your womb. *I have to go, Jayla. Call you later.*

You'd already guessed, but had chosen not to know. Jayla, you saw now, had been dropping sadistic little clues. It had been happening since soon after you'd told Charles he was going to be a dad. Apparently that title had scared him enough that he decided to substitute another: adulterer. On a hunch now you called Charles's just-for-you-or-emergencies cellphone—tied up—then Jayla's—the same. An hour later you made an appointment and that same day walked to the clinic with a hurricane inside your head and you faked composure and lied about how thoroughly you'd reflected and you signed the forms with a steady hand, had the ultrasound, embarked on the procedure—it was no miscarriage, except maybe in some metaphorical way—and minutes later you were sobbing unstoppably, spasm by spasm feeling your lover and your best friend purged out of you along with the baby-to-be. Best *friend?* In the stirrups you admitted not only that you'd been the sidekick, the loyal turnspit (you already knew that, of course), but that Jayla had always flirted aggressively with your boyfriends, needing to prove to herself, and maybe to you, that deep down they found her more attractive (how could they not?) and she could win them away from you at any time; they remained yours only out of her immense benevolence. As your body hemorrhaged Charles and your briefer history, you realized with self-disgust how terribly you'd duped yourself about him—how you'd shrugged off erotic dissatisfactions and your recurrent scorn at his pomposities as if these were just puny blips you could work around. In fact, in that hour of emphatic wakefulness, you saw that for months now you'd been sedating your awareness, somnambulating through relationships you were not so much trying to will as to *dream* into lasting rightness.

You returned, gutted, and collapsed in your bachelorette. Sent Charles a last email: *Baby gone. Say nothing to anyone. Say nothing more to me. "Vehemently," R.*

A vile, acrid paste spreads across your palate and your throat, starting to seal it like a diphtheria membrane. When you half wake, the flavour in your mouth is a milder version of that taste. Processional geometric dreams, like dreams in high fever. A dream of triangles, V-shaped torsos, deltas of androgynous pubic hair, pup tents of old canvas with humid, mildewy interiors. A cut-out creature with wedge-shaped body leglessly running in space. The stress horse? Sad seahorse, flushed by a tide of tears from the womb of its one chance. *I am sorry.* Your cot is teetered so your head is down, feet near the ceiling. Your bunkmate has augured a hole through the upper mattress. The hole is smooth and clean as if the mattress is solid pine. An eye peering. Your "paranoid" intuition is right, your bunkmate is a *man.* Of course. Enrol as a woman in a sedative trial and "sleep" in a dorm full of potential victims. Just pretend to swallow the pills. . . . You have to get out. You try to rise but you lie rigid, teeth gritted, a coffined cadaver. Try to call out a warning but your larynx has been excised by Dr. Wall. Your mouth gapes. The springs of the upper bunk scream.

You wake in shudders, staring up. By the light of Henry's Moon you see the upper bunk is unsagging, vacant. And someone is afoot in the room, moving softly.

"Stop!" you call out. Why has your voice shrunk to zero? You're still paralyzed—can't even open your eyes.

A firm hand on your shoulder.

"No!"

"Dear? Miss Kanakis? Are you all right?"

It's Nurse Nkwele, her brow-lamp lasering down, a mother ship returning.

"I thought you were the man above me," you blurt. "From the bunk above me."

"Man?" She sounds so weary, so unsurprised. "You have been having a dream."

"Where is he?"

"Gone, they took her downtown. Earlier in the night. She never should have been permitted to enrol." Nurse Nkwele sits beside you. "She was ill, that woman. I should not be telling you this."

"Thank God. I mean—thank God he . . . What did she have?"

"Judging by how she presented, a malarial condition. She has been doing volunteer work in Central America, on and off. I suppose she needed to make some quick money here. If I were to diagnose, she was having a mild relapse at the time she arrived, and the drugs, reducing her resistance, triggered a worse one."

"You're a doctor, aren't you? Not a nurse."

"I am a nurse. But you are correct."

Correct—that word people use when they want to confirm that you're right but keep their distance.

"My Nigerian credentials are not sufficient here. This night shift pays decently. In a few years, I'll go back to school here. Another two or three years of school." She straightens and stiffens. "I will have that blood now."

"May I ask a question?" It seems easy here in the night dorm, Nkwele's face anonymized under her blinding lamp and you essentially stoned.

"So long as your question is less personal. I have said more than is professional."

"It is personal," you say, "but it's not about you. Ouch," you add.

"Ask."

"Can love just happen, or do we always choose?"

Nurse Nkwele sighs. "Example, please."

"Your lover and your best friend, say. Love just happens to them, they can't choose not to be in love, so they are in love. And they do act."

She chuckles softly. "Such a North American idea, that. No. I would say that in such a case, there is always malice. Malice, not love. Malice in masquerade as love. Or a desire for power, in masquerade. So many things pretend to be love, do they not? The trick is not to believe the outer symptoms."

"That's more or less what I think," you say. "What I've decided. Thank you."

"Are you all right, girl?"

"I don't know."

"Here," she says, "let me tape you. You try to sleep now. Many of you seem to be having bad dreams."

Under the doctor's blue eyes the skin is bruised and pouchy, but the eyes themselves have a morning freshness. As you enter, he grins, almost shyly—a boy working up his nerve to ask a girl to the prom. It's creepy, yet touching. Even if his interest in you is clinical and close to morbid, it's touching.

"Hey, Roddy! You look better this morning. How do you feel?"

"Like I'm half asleep and just dreaming I'm here."

"Great. Just roll up your sleeve. Should we try first for a true reading?"

"Well, it might be harder for me to raise the pressure today," you say—and it's true, you do feel somewhat calmer, clearer, as if a fever has broken in the night.

He pumps, releases, eyes fixed to the gauge.

"You're not thinking about him now, to raise the numbers?"

"Not really."

"Because we're still low, but we're approaching low-normal." He reaches for his clipboard, looking shy again. "How would you feel about me, uh . . . doing a little follow-up on you, after this trial is done? I'm thinking of trying to write a small paper."

Now you place it, that faint, skunky smell: pot.

"What went wrong in that other sedative trial?" you ask.

"It's confidential, I'm afraid."

"I won't tell anyone."

He says eagerly, "A depressed male in dormitory B overdosed on a benzodiazepine variative we were retesting. Apparently that was his plan. He'd been suicidal on and off for a year and no longer had access to sleeping pills. He managed to bribe one of the other males to save his pills, every second one—just pretend to take them. Meanwhile he was doing the same. We noticed irregularities in the various blood tests, but the drug was new and we weren't sure what was happening. And this was before Vivienne. Nurse Nkwele. She's unfoolable. So after the last blood draw on the fourth night—sedative trials were five days then—he swallowed all the pills he'd stored up."

"He died?"

"But these things have a much lower toxicity than the old barbiturates. We figure he took at least fifteen. As expected, he just slept for a long time."

You gaze expectantly at Dr. Wall. He's enjoying himself.

"Eighty-two hours, to be exact!"

"A coma," you say.

"Ah, but the research indicates that drug-induced stupors are not the same as comas caused by accidents, say, or blunt trauma! It's something else I'd love to be researching, if I had the time. Last I heard, our Rumpelstiltskin was functioning again and hadn't repeated his attempt. Maybe we could all use a good eighty-hour sleep, huh?"

"Rip van Winkle," you say.

"Sorry?"

Something comes to you now, a poem you read in high school about kids climbing birch saplings until the young trees bend under their weight and deposit them back on the ground, and the poet brings it around to a wish that he might leave the earth for a while—take a little time off—then return and start over.

You wake at noon to a dormitory that no longer feels like an opium den. Less than twenty-four hours left. The atmosphere: like a classroom on the second-last

day of school, mid-June, the air tender, teachers leni-
ent, bullies lazy. A smell of coffee. The cafeteria brew,
dispensed in polystyrene cups, tastes like instant decaf,
but now the smell is palatable, even appealing.

Wen is sitting on her bunk, chatting with Sunetra
across the room. Han is on her cellphone talking to her
boyfriend—that's plain. Her voice is inaudible but her
face is a billet-doux. Eleanor is helping Hong again and
now even Ruth the cranky paralegal is involved.

Hong, a terrible newsprint colour but still diligent,
reads out another verse, something about violence no
longer being heard in the land, nor wasting nor destruc-
tion within the borders. She says, "I understand not this
wasting. Not like the garbage? Or spendthrift?"

"Hmm," says Eleanor. "That's a toughie. I think
maybe it means no more good things will be wasted.
What do you think, Ruth?"

"I love you tons, Rick," Han whispers under the
ambient bustle. "Tons." She looks as though she might
weep—and this doesn't destroy you.

Ruth is talking now, talking like someone who has
been trapped solo in a mineshaft for a month and is
spilling out her tale. Today's the first day she has felt
able to talk, she says. The cravings are easing off—for
a smoke. The work, she says, is high pressure and it
never backs off. "Never felt I could work without a
cigarette. I figured if I came out here and quit cold
turkey and slept for three days, through the worst of
the craving . . ."

"And now you're through it, aren't you?" Eleanor says.

"Getting there. Plus, I knew it would be hard to get smokes here."

"You could've bummed off me," Wen says, entering the conversation late and missing the point. "I was going outside for one now and then."

"I know, I could smell it on you. That's why I wouldn't talk to you."

"I quit smoking once," you announce. "It was the second hardest week of my life."

"What was the hardest?" Wen asks.

"Tough question," you say.

"Anyway," Ruth says, "I can see my way clear." Her hands are folded tightly in her lap. Han whispering, *Don't worry, I don't think I'll go back this summer.* Her accent revives some, though it doesn't seem conscious. *One summer of London was enough.*

"*My* hardest was last week," says Wen. "My boyfriends found out about each other. I'm kind of like . . . hiding out now. What about you, Sun?"

Sunetra's cheeks and ears darken. "Oh, it's too much like asking what's my favourite kind of wart. Are you scared they'll come after you?"

"They should cool off after a couple of days."

"It was when my father died," says Eleanor. "It was recently."

"I thought you said you were taking care of him," says Ruth.

"Oh, did I?"

In the silence, Hong shakes her head—not Job-like but with a bemused air—and says, "Too many hardest to pick one."

"I was," Eleanor says. "I'm sorry. It's such a thing when somebody dies under your care! I mean, when you have convinced yourself you can keep him alive. I always thought I should have been a nurse, not a secretary. Now I'm neither. I'm no longer a daughter, either. It's something you'll notice about aging. One by one, your . . . your . . . what is the word now, Roddy? Your *attributes*, they are withdrawn. Finally, I guess, you're nothing but yourself."

"Then not even that," Ruth says.

And you think: to be stripped down that way, at least for a brief period, might not be all bad. You say simply, "I'm sorry for your loss," and the others nod and murmur concurrence and you feel that in this moment—shortly before going your separate roads— the seven of you have become a group.

You wander out into the hallway, hungry at last. Is the bitter taste going, or are you just getting used to it? The *moussaka* is out of the question but you might try the special. Hot turkey sandwich with baked potato and peas. You pass the lone window and it hits you— swallows eat insects and migrate to warm, brighter places for the winter. The bird you saw before must have been a figment caused by the drug, a waking dream . . . You order and go to the payphone and dial your uncle at the restaurant. You don't think you can face waitressing for him again, but you know he pays his cooks decently and you're going to have to start saving. Nurse Nkwele, though she appears old to you—forty, at least—seems undaunted by the prospect of going back to school for another two or three years, or more. And this shames you a little, shakes you up.

"Roddy!" Uncle Lambros cries with heartbreaking joy. "It's you!"

[NOTES & ACKNOWLEDGEMENTS]

Some of the stories in this collection have been previously published in magazines and anthologies. The author is very grateful to the editors.

"Those Who Would Be More" appeared, as "Dialogues of Departure," in the United States in *Tin House* and in Canada in *The New Quarterly*.

"A Right Like Yours" appeared in the United States in *The Black Boot* and in Canada in *Maisonneuve* and was anthologized in *The Exile Book of Canadian Sports Stories* (Exile Editions, ed. Priscila Uppal). It appeared also in Douglas Glover's online magazine, *Numéro Cinq*.

"Shared Room on Union" appeared in *The Fiddlehead* and was anthologized in *2010: Best Canadian Stories* (Oberon, ed. John Metcalf). The story received the 2009 gold National Magazine Award for Fiction.

"OutTrip" appeared in *The Malahat Review*.

"The Dead Are More Visible" appeared in *The Walrus* and in *The Albawtaka Review* (Egypt); it was anthologized as an audio story on *Earlit Shorts* (ed. Susan Rendell and Janet Russell). The story received the 2007 gold National Magazine Award for Fiction.

"Noughts & Crosses" appeared in *The Walrus* and was anthologized in *The White Collar Book* (Black Moss Press, eds. Bruce Meyer and Carolyn Meyer).

"Fireman's Carry" appeared in *Geist*.

"Heart & Arrow" was first published in the United States in *The Northwest Review* and in Canada in the short-story collection *On earth as it is* (Porcupine's Quill, 1995; Granta Books, 1997; Vintage Canada, 2001). It appears in this book in a different, somewhat shorter form.

"Nearing the Sea, Superior" appeared in *Descant* and was anthologized in *2012: Best Canadian Stories* (Oberon, ed. John Metcalf).

As always, I thank my family and friends. Let me list with gratitude the names of people who have made specific contributions to this book over the past few years, whether by reading drafts of individual stories or by talking over ideas with me: Mary Huggard, Rich Cumyn, Grace O'Connell, Jared Bland, Judith Cowan, Mark Sinnett, Ingrid Ruthig, Sandra Ridley, Michael Holmes, Angie Abdou, Alvin Lee, John Metcalf, Jenny Haysom, Ginger Pharand, Tim Conley, Michael Winter, Michael Redhill, Alexander Scala, Alison Pick, Natalee Caple, Rachel Sa, and Jane Warren.

Thanks to Sue Sumeraj, again, for her exacting eye.

Special thanks to Anne McDermid, Martha Magor, and Monica Pacheco of Anne McDermid & Associates.

Above all, I wish to thank my editor, Amanda Lewis.

THOSE WHO WOULD BE MORE

In 1992 the Porcupine's Quill published a book of my short stories called *Flight Paths of the Emperor*—stories set mainly in Japan. For the next decade or so, I kept feeling that I should have written another story for the book; there were three bits of Japanese material that I regretted never having used (one being my experience of learning Japanese from a bizarre primer possibly authored by a psychopath), but none of these strands of narrative DNA seemed enough, in itself, to tease out into a story. Nor could I see any way of braiding them together. Then, a few years ago, I figured it out. Raising a daughter was probably the main thing that made the braiding possible, but I don't say that with any certainty, and in fact I'll say nothing more on the subject. It's disingenuous for fiction writers to pretend they know how their stories really gestate.

A RIGHT LIKE YOURS

Some years ago I ran across a website brilliantly called *Runs With Dog*—hence my idea for the name of the dog (Runs With Man) in this story.

OUTTRIP

For their assistance and advice, I am indebted to Arlen Baptiste, of the Nk'Mip Desert Cultural Centre, and his grandfather, Richard Armstrong, of the En'owkin Centre, Penticton, BC. These knowledgeable men are not responsible for the presence of coywolves—properly an Eastern phenomenon—in my hallucinatory version of the Okanagan Desert.

FIREMAN'S CARRY

My thanks to firefighter Doug Caldwell for carefully checking over the story.

STEVEN HEIGHTON is the author of the novel *Every Lost Country*, which was a national bestseller, a *Globe and Mail*, *Amazon.ca* and *Maisonneuve* Best Book, and a finalist for the Banff Mountain Book Award, and which has been optioned for film. His novel *Afterlands* appeared in six countries, was a *New York Times Book Review* Editors' Choice as well as a Best Book of the Year selection in ten publications in Canada, the United States, and Britain, and has been optioned for film. He also wrote *The Shadow Boxer*, a Canadian bestseller and a *Publishers Weekly* Book of the Year. His work has been translated into ten languages, and his poems and stories have appeared in the *London Review of Books*, *Poetry*, *Tin House*, *The Walrus*, *Best American Poetry*, *TLR*, *Agni*, *Brick*, *Best English Stories*, and many others. Heighton has received four gold and one silver National Magazine awards (for fiction and poetry) and has been nominated for the Governor General's Literary Award, the Trillium Award, a Pushcart Prize, and Britain's W.H. Smith Award. Visit his website at www.stevenheighton.com.

[A NOTE ABOUT THE TYPE]

The principle text of *The Dead Are More Visible* has been set in Janson, a misnamed typeface designed in or about 1690 by Nicholas Kis, a Hungarian in Amsterdam. In 1919 the original matrices became the property of the Stempel Foundry in Frankfurt, Germany. Janson is an old-style book face of excellent clarity and sharpness, featuring concave and splayed serifs, and a marked contrast between thick and thin strokes.